THE WORKS OF
HENRY VAN DYKE
AVALON EDITION

VOLUME IX

POEMS

I

Henry van Dyke
From a photograph by A. F. Bradley

i

POEMS

BY
HENRY VAN DYKE

VOLUME ONE

NEW YORK
CHARLES SCRIBNER'S SONS
1920

Copyright, 1900, 1904, 1908, 1909, 1911, 1914, 1915, 1916, 1917, 1918, 1919, 1920,
by Charles Scribner's Sons

Copyright, 1913, 1914, 1916, 1917, 1918, by Harper & Brothers
Copyright, 1913, by Life Publishing Company
Copyright, 1918, by P. F. Collier & Son, Inc.
Copyright, 1915, 1916, 1918, by the Outlook Company
Copyright, 1916, by American Academy of Arts and Letters
Copyright, 1916, by the Kalon Publishing Co., Inc.
Copyright, 1917, by The Independent
Copyright, 1917, by The New York Times Company
Copyright, 1918, by The New York Herald Co.
Copyright, 1918, by New York Tribune, Inc.
Copyright, 1917, by Land and Water Publishing Co.
Copyright, 1918, by The Public Ledger
Copyright, 1918, by The Press Publishing Co.

To
KATRINA TRASK

CONTENTS

SONGS OUT OF DOORS
EARLY VERSES

The After-Echo	3
Dulciora	4
Three Alpine Sonnets	6
Matins	9
The Parting and the Coming Guest	10
If All the Skies	12
Wings of a Dove	13
The Fall of the Leaves	14
A Snow-Song	16
Roslin and Hawthornden	17

SONGS OUT OF DOORS
LATER POEMS

When Tulips Bloom	21
The Whip-Poor-Will	24
The Lily of Yorrow	27
The Veery	29
The Song-Sparrow	31
The Maryland Yellow-Throat	33
A November Daisy	35
The Angler's Reveille	37
The Ruby-Crowned Kinglet	41

CONTENTS

School	45
Indian Summer	46
Spring in the North	47
Spring in the South	51
A Noon Song	53
Light Between the Trees	55
The Hermit Thrush	57
Turn o' the Tide	58
Sierra Madre	59
The Grand Canyon	61
The Heavenly Hills of Holland	67
Flood-Tide of Flowers	69
God of the Open Air	71

NARRATIVE POEMS

The Toiling of Felix	81
Vera	101
Another Chance	120
A Legend of Service	125
The White Bees	129
New Year's Eve	137
The Vain King	142
The Foolish Fir-Tree	147
"Gran' Boule"	151
Heroes of the "Titanic"	157
The Standard-Bearer	158
The Proud Lady	159

CONTENTS

LABOUR AND ROMANCE

A Mile with Me	165
The Three Best Things	166
Reliance	169
Doors of Daring	170
The Child in the Garden	171
Love's Reason	172
The Echo in the Heart	173
"Undine"	174
"Rencontre"	175
Love in a Look	177
My April Lady	178
A Lover's Envy	179
Fire-Fly City	180
The Gentle Traveller	182
Nepenthe	183
Day and Night	185
Hesper	186
Arrival	187
Departure	188
The Black Birds	189
Without Disguise	192
An Hour	193
"Rappelle-Toi"	194
Love's Nearness	196
Two Songs of Heine	197

CONTENTS

Eight Echoes from the Poems of Auguste Angellier	198
Rappel d'Amour	209
The River of Dreams	210

HEARTH AND ALTAR

A Home Song	217
"Little Boatie"	218
A Mother's Birthday	220
Transformation	222
Rendezvous	223
Gratitude	224
Peace	225
Santa Christina	226
The Bargain	229
To the Child Jesus	230
Bitter-Sweet	231
Hymn of Joy	232
Song of a Pilgrim-Soul	234
Ode to Peace	235
Three Prayers for Sleep and Waking	239
Portrait and Reality	242
The Wind of Sorrow	243
Hide and Seek	244
Autumn in the Garden	246
The Message	248
Dulcis Memoria	249

CONTENTS

The Window	251
Christmas Tears	253
Dorothea, 1888–1912	255

EPIGRAMS, GREETINGS, AND INSCRIPTIONS

For Katrina's Sun-Dial	259
For Katrina's Window	260
For the Friends at Hurstmont	261
The Sun-Dial at Morven	263
The Sun-Dial at Wells College	263
To Mark Twain	264
Stars and the Soul	266
To Julia Marlowe	268
To Joseph Jefferson	268
The Mocking-Bird	269
The Empty Quatrain	269
Pan Learns Music	270
The Shepherd of Nymphs	270
Echoes from the Greek Anthology	271
One World	274
Joy and Duty	274
The Prison and the Angel	275
The Way	275
Love and Light	276
Facta non Verba	276
Four Things	277

CONTENTS

The Great River	277
Inscription for a Tomb in England	278
The Talisman	279
Thorn and Rose	280
"The Signs"	281

SONGS OUT OF DOORS
EARLY VERSES

THE AFTER-ECHO

How long the echoes love to play
  Around the shore of silence, as a wave
  Retreating circles down the sand!
  One after one, with sweet delay,
The mellow sounds that cliff and island gave,
  Have lingered in the crescent bay,
  Until, by lightest breezes fanned,
They float far off beyond the dying day
    And leave it still as death.
    But hark,—
  Another singing breath
  Comes from the edge of dark;
    A note as clear and slow
  As falls from some enchanted bell,
  Or spirit, passing from the world below,
    That whispers back, Farewell.

    So in the heart,
  When, fading slowly down the past,
    Fond memories depart,
  And each that leaves it seems the last;
  Long after all the rest are flown,
  Returns a solitary tone,—
  The after-echo of departed years,—
  And touches all the soul to tears.

1871.

DULCIORA

A TEAR that trembles for a little while
Upon the trembling eyelid, till the world
Wavers within its circle like a dream,
Holds more of meaning in its narrow orb
Than all the distant landscape that it blurs.

A smile that hovers round a mouth beloved,
Like the faint pulsing of the Northern Light,
And grows in silence to an amber dawn
Born in the sweetest depths of trustful eyes,
Is dearer to the soul than sun or star.

A joy that falls into the hollow heart
From some far-lifted height of love unseen,
Unknown, makes a more perfect melody
Than hidden brooks that murmur in the dusk,
Or fall athwart the cliff with wavering gleam.

Ah, not for their own sake are earth and sky
And the fair ministries of Nature dear,
But as they set themselves unto the tune
That fills our life; as light mysterious
Flows from within and glorifies the world.

DULCIORA

For so a common wayside blossom, touched
With tender thought, assumes a grace more sweet
Than crowns the royal lily of the South;
And so a well-remembered perfume seems
The breath of one who breathes in Paradise.

1872.

THREE ALPINE SONNETS

I

THE GLACIER

At dawn in silence moves the mighty stream,
  The silver-crested waves no murmur make;
  But far away the avalanches wake
The rumbling echoes, dull as in a dream;
Their momentary thunders, dying, seem
  To fall into the stillness, flake by flake,
  And leave the hollow air with naught to break
The frozen spell of solitude supreme.

At noon unnumbered rills begin to spring
  Beneath the burning sun, and all the walls
Of all the ocean-blue crevasses ring
  With liquid lyrics of their waterfalls;
As if a poet's heart had felt the glow
Of sovereign love, and song began to flow.

Zermatt, 1872.

THREE ALPINE SONNETS

II

THE SNOW-FIELD

White Death had laid his pall upon the plain,
   And crowned the mountain-peaks like monarchs dead;
   The vault of heaven was glaring overhead
With pitiless light that filled my eyes with pain;
And while I vainly longed, and looked in vain
   For sign or trace of life, my spirit said,
   "Shall any living thing that dares to tread
This royal lair of Death escape again?"

But even then I saw before my feet
   A line of pointed footprints in the snow:
   Some roving chamois, but an hour ago,
Had passed this way along his journey fleet,
And left a message from a friend unknown
To cheer my pilgrim-heart, no more alone.

Zermatt, 1872.

SONGS OUT OF DOORS

III

MOVING BELLS

I love the hour that comes, with dusky hair
   And dewy feet, along the Alpine dells,
   To lead the cattle forth. A thousand bells
Go chiming after her across the fair
And flowery uplands, while the rosy flare
   Of sunset on the snowy mountain dwells,
   And valleys darken, and the drowsy spells
Of peace are woven through the purple air.

Dear is the magic of this hour: she seems
   To walk before the dark by falling rills,
And lend a sweeter song to hidden streams;
   She opens all the doors of night, and fills
With moving bells the music of my dreams,
   That wander far among the sleeping hills.

Gstaad, August, 1909.

MATINS

FLOWERS rejoice when night is done,
Lift their heads to greet the sun;
Sweetest looks and odours raise,
In a silent hymn of praise.

So my heart would turn away
From the darkness to the day;
Lying open in God's sight
Like a flower in the light.

THE PARTING AND THE COMING GUEST

WHO watched the worn-out Winter die?
   Who, peering through the window-pane
   At nightfall, under sleet and rain
Saw the old graybeard totter by?
Who listened to his parting sigh,
   The sobbing of his feeble breath,
   His whispered colloquy with Death,
   And when his all of life was done
Stood near to bid a last good-bye?
   Of all his former friends not one
Saw the forsaken Winter die.

Who welcomed in the maiden Spring?
   Who heard her footfall, swift and light
   As fairy-dancing in the night?
Who guessed what happy dawn would bring
The flutter of her bluebird's wing,
The blossom of her mayflower-face
   To brighten every shady place?
   One morning, down the village street,
"Oh, here am I," we heard her sing,—
   And none had been awake to greet
The coming of the maiden Spring.

THE PARTING AND THE COMING GUEST

But look, her violet eyes are wet
  With bright, unfallen, dewy tears;
  And in her song my fancy hears
A note of sorrow trembling yet.
Perhaps, beyond the town, she met
  Old Winter as he limped away
  To die forlorn, and let him lay
  His weary head upon her knee,
  And kissed his forehead with regret
  For one so gray and lonely,—see,
Her eyes with tender tears are wet.

And so, by night, while we were all at rest,
I think the coming sped the parting guest.

1873.

IF ALL THE SKIES

If all the skies were sunshine,
  Our faces would be fain
To feel once more upon them
  The cooling plash of rain.

If all the world were music,
  Our hearts would often long
For one sweet strain of silence,
  To break the endless song.

If life were always merry,
  Our souls would seek relief,
And rest from weary laughter
  In the quiet arms of grief.

WINGS OF A DOVE

I

At sunset, when the rosy light was dying
  Far down the pathway of the west,
I saw a lonely dove in silence flying,
      To be at rest.

Pilgrim of air, I cried, could I but borrow
  Thy wandering wings, thy freedom blest,
I'd fly away from every careful sorrow,
      And find my rest.

II

But when the filmy veil of dusk was falling,
  Home flew the dove to seek his nest,
Deep in the forest where his mate was calling
      To love and rest.

Peace, heart of mine! no longer sigh to wander;
  Lose not thy life in barren quest.
There are no happy islands over yonder;
      Come home and rest.

1874.

THE FALL OF THE LEAVES

I

In warlike pomp, with banners flowing,
  The regiments of autumn stood:
I saw their gold and scarlet glowing
  From every hillside, every wood.

Above the sea the clouds were keeping
  Their secret leaguer, gray and still;
They sent their misty vanguard creeping
  With muffled step from hill to hill.

All day the sullen armies drifted
  Athwart the sky with slanting rain;
At sunset for a space they lifted,
  With dusk they settled down again.

II

At dark the winds began to blow
With mutterings distant, low;
  From sea and sky they called their strength,
    Till with an angry, broken roar,
    Like billows on an unseen shore,
Their fury burst at length.

THE FALL OF THE LEAVES

I heard through the night
  The rush and the clamour;
The pulse of the fight
  Like blows of Thor's hammer;
The pattering flight
Of the leaves, and the anguished
Moan of the forest vanquished.

At daybreak came a gusty song:
"Shout! the winds are strong.
The little people of the leaves are fled.
Shout! The Autumn is dead!"

III

The storm is ended! The impartial sun
Laughs down upon the battle lost and won,
And crowns the triumph of the cloudy host
In rolling lines retreating to the coast.

But we, fond lovers of the woodland shade,
And grateful friends of every fallen leaf,
Forget the glories of the cloud-parade,
And walk the ruined woods in quiet grief.

For ever so our thoughtful hearts repeat
On fields of triumph dirges of defeat;
And still we turn on gala-days to tread
Among the rustling memories of the dead.
1874.

A SNOW-SONG

Does the snow fall at sea?
  Yes, when the north winds blow,
  When the wild clouds fly low,
  Out of each gloomy wing,
  Silently glimmering,
  Over the stormy sea
    Falleth the snow.

Does the snow hide the sea?
  Nay, on the tossing plains
  Never a flake remains;
  Drift never resteth there;
  Vanishing everywhere,
  Into the hungry sea
    Falleth the snow.

What means the snow at sea?
  Whirled in the veering blast,
  Thickly the flakes drive past;
  Each like a childish ghost
  Wavers, and then is lost;
  In the forgetful sea
    Fadeth the snow.

1875.

ROSLIN AND HAWTHORNDEN

Fair Roslin Chapel, how divine
The art that reared thy costly shrine!
Thy carven columns must have grown
By magic, like a dream in stone.

Yet not within thy storied wall
Would I in adoration fall,
So gladly as within the glen
That leads to lovely Hawthornden.

A long-drawn aisle, with roof of green
And vine-clad pillars, while between,
The Esk runs murmuring on its way,
In living music night and day.

Within the temple of this wood
The martyrs of the covenant stood,
And rolled the psalm, and poured the prayer,
From Nature's solemn altar-stair.

Edinburgh, 1877.

SONGS OUT OF DOORS
LATER POEMS

WHEN TULIPS BLOOM

I

When tulips bloom in Union Square,
And timid breaths of vernal air
  Go wandering down the dusty town,
Like children lost in Vanity Fair;

When every long, unlovely row
Of westward houses stands aglow,
  And leads the eyes to sunset skies
Beyond the hills where green trees grow;

Then weary seems the street parade,
And weary books, and weary trade:
  I'm only wishing to go a-fishing;
For this the month of May was made.

II

I guess the pussy-willows now
Are creeping out on every bough
  Along the brook; and robins look
For early worms behind the plough.

SONGS OUT OF DOORS

The thistle-birds have changed their dun,
For yellow coats, to match the sun;
　And in the same array of flame
The Dandelion Show's begun.

The flocks of young anemones
Are dancing round the budding trees:
　Who can help wishing to go a-fishing
In days as full of joy as these?

III

I think the meadow-lark's clear sound
Leaks upward slowly from the ground,
　While on the wing the bluebirds ring
Their wedding-bells to woods around.

The flirting chewink calls his dear
Behind the bush; and very near,
　Where water flows, where green grass grows,
Song-sparrows gently sing, "Good cheer."

And, best of all, through twilight's calm
The hermit-thrush repeats his psalm.
　How much I'm wishing to go a-fishing
In days so sweet with music's balm!

WHEN TULIPS BLOOM

IV

'Tis not a proud desire of mine;
I ask for nothing superfine;
  No heavy weight, no salmon great,
To break the record, or my line.

Only an idle little stream,
Whose amber waters softly gleam,
  Where I may wade through woodland shade,
And cast the fly, and loaf, and dream:

Only a trout or two, to dart
From foaming pools, and try my art:
  'Tis all I'm wishing—old-fashioned fishing,
And just a day on Nature's heart.

1894.

THE WHIP-POOR-WILL

Do you remember, father,—
    It seems so long ago,—
The day we fished together
    Along the Pocono?
At dusk I waited for you,
    Beside the lumber-mill,
And there I heard a hidden bird
    That chanted, "whip-poor-will,"
    "Whippoorwill! whippoorwill!"
Sad and shrill,—*"whippoorwill!"*

The place was all deserted;
    The mill-wheel hung at rest;
The lonely star of evening
    Was throbbing in the west;
The veil of night was falling;
    The winds were folded still;
And everywhere the trembling air
    Re-echoed "whip-poor-will!"
    "Whippoorwill! whippoorwill!"
Sad and shrill,—*"whippoorwill!"*

You seemed so long in coming,
    I felt so much alone;
The wide, dark world was round me,
    And life was all unknown;

THE WHIP-POOR-WILL

The hand of sorrow touched me,
  And made my senses thrill
With all the pain that haunts the strain
  Of mournful whip-poor-will.
  "Whippoorwill! whippoorwill!"
  Sad and shrill,—*"whippoorwill!"*

What knew I then of trouble?
  An idle little lad,
I had not learned the lessons
  That make men wise and sad.
I dreamed of grief and parting,
  And something seemed to fill
My heart with tears, while in my ears
  Resounded "whip-poor-will."
  "Whippoorwill! whippoorwill!"
  Sad and shrill,—*"whippoorwill!"*

'Twas but a cloud of sadness,
  That lightly passed away;
But I have learned the meaning
  Of sorrow, since that day.
For nevermore at twilight,
  Beside the silent mill,
I'll wait for you, in the falling dew,
  And hear the whip-poor-will.
  "Whippoorwill! whippoorwill!"
  Sad and shrill,—*"whippoorwill!"*

SONGS OUT OF DOORS

But if you still remember
   In that fair land of light,
The pains and fears that touch us
   Along this edge of night,
I think all earthly grieving,
   And all our mortal ill,
To you must seem like a sad boy's dream,
   Who hears the whip-poor-will.
   "*Whippoorwill! whippoorwill!*"
   A passing thrill,—"*whippoorwill!*"

1894.

THE LILY OF YORROW

Deep in the heart of the forest the lily of Yorrow is growing;
Blue is its cup as the sky, and with mystical odour o'erflowing;
Faintly it falls through the shadowy glades when the south wind is blowing.

Sweet are the primroses pale and the violets after a shower;
Sweet are the borders of pinks and the blossoming grapes on the bower;
Sweeter by far is the breath of that far-away woodland flower.

Searching and strange in its sweetness, it steals like a perfume enchanted
Under the arch of the forest, and all who perceive it are haunted,
Seeking and seeking for ever, till sight of the lily is granted.

Who can describe how it grows, with its chalice of lazuli leaning
Over a crystalline spring, where the ferns and the mosses are greening?
Who can imagine its beauty, or utter the depth of its meaning?

SONGS OUT OF DOORS

Calm of the journeying stars, and repose of the mountains olden,
Joy of the swift-running rivers, and glory of sunsets golden,
Secrets that cannot be told in the heart of the flower are holden.

Surely to see it is peace and the crown of a life-long endeavour;
Surely to pluck it is gladness,—but they who have found it can never
Tell of the gladness and peace: they are hid from our vision for ever.

'Twas but a moment ago that a comrade was walking near me:
Turning aside from the pathway he murmured a greeting to cheer me,—
Then he was lost in the shade, and I called but he did not hear me.

Why should I dream he is dead, and bewail him with passionate sorrow?
Surely I know there is gladness in finding the lily of Yorrow:
He has discovered it first, and perhaps I shall find it to-morrow.

1894.

THE VEERY

The moonbeams over Arno's vale in silver flood were pouring,
When first I heard the nightingale a long-lost love deploring.
So passionate, so full of pain, it sounded strange and eerie;
I longed to hear a simpler strain,—the wood-notes of the veery.

The laverock sings a bonny lay above the Scottish heather;
It sprinkles down from far away like light and love together;
He drops the golden notes to greet his brooding mate, his dearie;
I only know one song more sweet,—the vespers of the veery.

In English gardens, green and bright and full of fruity treasure,
I heard the blackbird with delight repeat his merry measure:
The ballad was a pleasant one, the tune was loud and cheery,
And yet, with every setting sun, I listened for the veery.

SONGS OUT OF DOORS

But far away, and far away, the tawny thrush is singing;
New England woods, at close of day, with that clear
    chant are ringing:
And when my light of life is low, and heart and flesh
    are weary,
I fain would hear, before I go, the wood-notes of the
    veery.

1895.

THE SONG-SPARROW

There is a bird I know so well,
   It seems as if he must have sung
   Beside my crib when I was young;
Before I knew the way to spell
   The name of even the smallest bird,
   His gentle-joyful song I heard.
Now see if you can tell, my dear,
What bird it is that, every year,
Sings "*Sweet—sweet—sweet—very merry cheer.*"

He comes in March, when winds are strong,
   And snow returns to hide the earth;
   But still he warms his heart with mirth,
And waits for May. He lingers long
   While flowers fade; and every day
   Repeats his small, contented lay;
As if to say, we need not fear
The season's change, if love is here
With "*Sweet—sweet—sweet—very merry cheer.*"

He does not wear a Joseph's-coat
   Of many colours, smart and gay;
   His suit is Quaker brown and gray,
With darker patches at his throat.
   And yet of all the well-dressed throng

SONGS OUT OF DOORS

Not one can sing so brave a song.
It makes the pride of looks appear
A vain and foolish thing, to hear
His "*Sweet—sweet—sweet—very merry cheer.*"

A lofty place he does not love,
  But sits by choice, and well at ease,
  In hedges, and in little trees
That stretch their slender arms above
  The meadow-brook; and there he sings
  Till all the field with pleasure rings;
And so he tells in every ear,
That lowly homes to heaven are near
In "*Sweet—sweet—sweet—very merry cheer.*"

I like the tune, I like the words;
  They seem so true, so free from art,
  So friendly, and so full of heart,
That if but one of all the birds
  Could be my comrade everywhere,
  My little brother of the air,
I'd choose the song-sparrow, my dear,
Because he'd bless me, every year,
With "*Sweet—sweet—sweet—very merry cheer.*"
1895.

THE MARYLAND YELLOW-THROAT

When May bedecks the naked trees
With tassels and embroideries,
And many blue-eyed violets beam
Along the edges of the stream,
I hear a voice that seems to say,
Now near at hand, now far away,
   "Witchery—witchery—witchery."

An incantation so serene,
So innocent, befits the scene:
There's magic in that small bird's note—
See, there he flits—the Yellow-throat;
A living sunbeam, tipped with wings,
A spark of light that shines and sings
   "Witchery—witchery—witchery."

You prophet with a pleasant name,
If out of Mary-land you came,
You know the way that thither goes
Where Mary's lovely garden grows:
Fly swiftly back to her, I pray,
And try to call her down this way,
   "Witchery—witchery—witchery!"

SONGS OUT OF DOORS

Tell her to leave her cockle-shells,
And all her little silver bells
That blossom into melody,
And all her maids less fair than she.
She does not need these pretty things,
For everywhere she comes, she brings
   "*Witchery—witchery—witchery!*"

The woods are greening overhead,
And flowers adorn each mossy bed;
The waters babble as they run—
One thing is lacking, only one:
If Mary were but here to-day,
I would believe your charming lay,
   "*Witchery—witchery—witchery!*"

Along the shady road I look—
Who's coming now across the brook?
A woodland maid, all robed in white—
The leaves dance round her with delight,
The stream laughs out beneath her feet—
Sing, merry bird, the charm's complete,
   "*Witchery—witchery—witchery!*"

1895.

A NOVEMBER DAISY

Afterthought of summer's bloom!
Late arrival at the feast,
Coming when the songs have ceased
And the merry guests departed,
Leaving but an empty room,
Silence, solitude, and gloom,—
Are you lonely, heavy-hearted;
You, the last of all your kind,
Nodding in the autumn wind;
Now that all your friends are flown,
Blooming late and all alone?

Nay, I wrong you, little flower,
Reading mournful mood of mine
In your looks, that give no sign
Of a spirit dark and cheerless!
You possess the heavenly power
That rejoices in the hour.
Glad, contented, free, and fearless,
Lift a sunny face to heaven
When a sunny day is given!
Make a summer of your own,
Blooming late and all alone!

SONGS OUT OF DOORS

Once the daisies gold and white
Sea-like through the meadow rolled:
Once my heart could hardly hold
All its pleasures. I remember,
In the flood of youth's delight
Separate joys were lost to sight.
That was summer! Now November
Sets the perfect flower apart;
Gives each blossom of the heart
Meaning, beauty, grace unknown,—
Blooming late and all alone.

November, 1899.

THE ANGLER'S REVEILLE

WHAT time the rose of dawn is laid across the lips of night,
And all the little watchman-stars have fallen asleep in light,
'Tis then a merry wind awakes, and runs from tree to tree,
And borrows words from all the birds to sound the reveille.

    This is the carol the Robin throws
      Over the edge of the valley;
    Listen how boldly it flows,
      Sally on sally:
        Tirra-lirra,
        Early morn,
        New born!
        Day is near,
        Clear, clear.
        Down the river
        All a-quiver,
        Fish are breaking;
        Time for waking,
        Tup, tup, tup!
        Do you hear?
        All clear—
        Wake up!

SONGS OUT OF DOORS

The phantom flood of dreams has ebbed and vanished
    with the dark,
And like a dove the heart forsakes the prison of the ark;
Now forth she fares thro' friendly woods and diamond-
    fields of dew,
While every voice cries out "Rejoice!" as if the world
    were new.

    This is the ballad the Bluebird sings,
        Unto his mate replying,
    Shaking the tune from his wings
        While he is flying:
            Surely, surely, surely,
              Life is dear
              Even here.
              Blue above,
              You to love,
            Purely, purely, purely.

There's wild azalea on the hill, and iris down the dell,
And just one spray of lilac still abloom beside the well;
The columbine adorns the rocks, the laurel buds grow
    pink,
Along the stream white arums gleam, and violets bend
    to drink.

    This is the song of the Yellow-throat,
        Fluttering gaily beside you;

THE ANGLER'S REVEILLE

Hear how each voluble note
   Offers to guide you:
      Which way, sir?
      I say, sir,
      Let me teach you,
      I beseech you!
      Are you wishing
      Jolly fishing?
      This way, sir!
      I'll teach you.

Then come, my friend, forget your foes and leave your fears behind,
And wander forth to try your luck, with cheerful, quiet mind;
For be your fortune great or small, you take what God will give,
And all the day your heart will say, "'Tis luck enough to live."

   This is the song the Brown Thrush flings
     Out of his thicket of roses;
   Hark how it bubbles and rings,
     Mark how it closes:
      Luck, luck,
      What luck?
      Good enough for me,
      I'm alive, you see!

SONGS OUT OF DOORS

Sun shining,
No repining;
Never borrow
Idle sorrow;
Drop it!
Cover it up!
Hold your cup!
Joy will fill it,
Don't spill it,
Steady, be ready,
Good luck!

1899.

THE RUBY–CROWNED KINGLET

I

Where's your kingdom, little king?
  Where the land you call your own,
  Where your palace and your throne?
Fluttering lightly on the wing
  Through the blossom-world of May,
  Whither lies your royal way,
        Little king?

Far to northward lies a land
Where the trees together stand
Closely as the blades of wheat
When the summer is complete.
Rolling like an ocean wide
Over vale and mountainside,
Balsam, hemlock, spruce and pine,—
All those mighty trees are mine.
There's a river flowing free,—
All its waves belong to me.
There's a lake so clear and bright
Stars shine out of it all night;
Rowan-berries round it spread
Like a belt of coral red.
Never royal garden planned
Fair as my Canadian land!

SONGS OUT OF DOORS

There I build my summer nest,
There I reign and there I rest,
While from dawn to dark I sing,
Happy kingdom! Lucky king!

II

Back again, my little king!
  Is your happy kingdom lost
  To the rebel knave, Jack Frost?
Have you felt the snow-flakes sting?
  Houseless, homeless in October,
    Whither now? Your plight is sober,
      Exiled king!

Far to southward lie the regions
Where my loyal flower-legions
Hold possession of the year,
Filling every month with cheer.
Christmas wakes the winter rose;
New Year daffodils unclose;
Yellow jasmine through the wood
Flows in February flood,
Dropping from the tallest trees
Golden streams that never freeze.
Thither now I take my flight
Down the pathway of the night,
Till I see the southern moon

THE RUBY-CROWNED KINGLET

Glisten on the broad lagoon,
Where the cypress' dusky green,
And the dark magnolia's sheen,
Weave a shelter round my home.
There the snow-storms never come;
There the bannered mosses gray
Like a curtain gently sway,
Hanging low on every side
Round the covert where I bide,
Till the March azalea glows,
Royal red and heavenly rose,
Through the Carolina glade
Where my winter home is made.
There I hold my southern court,
Full of merriment and sport:
There I take my ease and sing,
Happy kingdom! Lucky king!

III

Little boaster, vagrant king,
  Neither north nor south is yours,
  You've no kingdom that endures!
Wandering every fall and spring,
With your ruby crown so slender,
Are you only a Pretender,
        Landless king?

SONGS OUT OF DOORS

Never king by right divine
Ruled a richer realm than mine!
What are lands and golden crowns,
Armies, fortresses and towns,
Jewels, sceptres, robes and rings,—
What are these to song and wings?
Everywhere that I can fly,
There I own the earth and sky;
Everywhere that I can sing.
There I'm happy as a king.

1900.

SCHOOL

I PUT my heart to school
In the world where men grow wise:
"Go out," I said, "and learn the rule;
"Come back when you win a prize."

My heart came back again:
"Now where is the prize?" I cried.—
"The rule was false, and the prize was pain,
"And the teacher's name was Pride."

I put my heart to school
In the woods where veeries sing
And brooks run clear and cool,
In the fields where wild flowers spring.

"And why do you stay so long
"My heart, and where do you roam?"
The answer came with a laugh and a song,—
"I find this school is home."

April, 1901.

INDIAN SUMMER

A SILKEN curtain veils the skies,
And half conceals from pensive eyes
  The bronzing tokens of the fall;
A calmness broods upon the hills,
And summer's parting dream distils
  A charm of silence over all.

The stacks of corn, in brown array,
Stand waiting through the tranquil day,
  Like tattered wigwams on the plain;
The tribes that find a shelter there
Are phantom peoples, forms of air,
  And ghosts of vanished joy and pain.

At evening when the crimson crest
Of sunset passes down the West,
  I hear the whispering host returning;
On far-off fields, by elm and oak,
I see the lights, I smell the smoke,—
  The Camp-fires of the Past are burning.

Tertius and Henry van Dyke.
November, 1903.

SPRING IN THE NORTH

I

AH, who will tell me, in these leaden days,
Why the sweet Spring delays,
And where she hides,—the dear desire
  Of every heart that longs
For bloom, and fragrance, and the ruby fire
Of maple-buds along the misty hills,
And that immortal call which fills
  The waiting wood with songs?
The snow-drops came so long ago,
  It seemed that Spring was near!
  But then returned the snow
With biting winds, and earth grew sere,
  And sullen clouds drooped low
To veil the sadness of a hope deferred:
Then rain, rain, rain, incessant rain
  Beat on the window-pane,
Through which I watched the solitary bird
That braved the tempest, buffeted and tossed
With rumpled feathers down the wind again.
  Oh, were the seeds all lost
When winter laid the wild flowers in their tomb?
  I searched the woods in vain
For blue hepaticas, and trilliums white,
And trailing arbutus, the Spring's delight,

SONGS OUT OF DOORS

Starring the withered leaves with rosy bloom.
　But every night the frost
To all my longing spoke a silent nay,
And told me Spring was far away.
Even the robins were too cold to sing,
Except a broken and discouraged note,—
Only the tuneful sparrow, on whose throat
Music has put her triple finger-print,
Lifted his head and sang my heart a hint,—
"Wait, wait, wait! oh, wait a while for Spring!"

II

But now, Carina, what divine amends
For all delay! What sweetness treasured up,
　What wine of joy that blends
A hundred flavours in a single cup,
Is poured into this perfect day!
For look, sweet heart, here are the early flowers
　That lingered on their way,
Thronging in haste to kiss the feet of May,
Entangled with the bloom of later hours,—
Anemones and cinque-foils, violets blue
And white, and iris richly gleaming through
The grasses of the meadow, and a blaze
Of butter-cups and daisies in the field,
　Filling the air with praise,
As if a chime of golden bells had pealed!

SPRING IN THE NORTH

The frozen songs within the breast
Of silent birds that hid in leafless woods,
  Melt into rippling floods
  Of gladness unrepressed.
Now oriole and bluebird, thrush and lark,
Warbler and wren and vireo,
Mingle their melody; the living spark
Of Love has touched the fuel of desire,
And every heart leaps up in singing fire.
  It seems as if the land
Were breathing deep beneath the sun's caress,
  Trembling with tenderness,
  While all the woods expand,
In shimmering clouds of rose and gold and green,
To veil a joy too sacred to be seen.

III

  Come, put your hand in mine,
True love, long sought and found at last,
And lead me deep into the Spring divine
  That makes amends for all the wintry past.
For all the flowers and songs I feared to miss
    Arrive with you;
And in the lingering pressure of your kiss
    My dreams come true;
And in the promise of your generous eyes
    I read the mystic sign

SONGS OUT OF DOORS

Of joy more perfect made
Because so long delayed,
And bliss enhanced by rapture of surprise.
Ah, think not early love alone is strong;
He loveth best whose heart has learned to wait:
Dear messenger of Spring that tarried long,
You're doubly dear because you come so late.

SPRING IN THE SOUTH

Now in the oak the sap of life is welling,
   Tho' to the bough the rusty leafage clings;
Now on the elm the misty buds are swelling;
   Every little pine-wood grows alive with wings;
Blue-jays are fluttering, yodeling and crying,
   Meadow-larks sailing low above the faded grass,
Red-birds whistling clear, silent robins flying,—
   Who has waked the birds up? What has come to pass?

Last year's cotton-plants, desolately bowing,
   Tremble in the March-wind, ragged and forlorn;
Red are the hillsides of the early ploughing,
   Gray are the lowlands, waiting for the corn.
Earth seems asleep, but she is only feigning;
   Deep in her bosom thrills a sweet unrest;
Look where the jasmine lavishly is raining
   Jove's golden shower into Danäe's breast!

Now on the plum-tree a snowy bloom is sifted,
   Now on the peach-tree, the glory of the rose,
Far o'er the hills a tender haze is drifted,
   Full to the brim the yellow river flows.
Dark cypress boughs with vivid jewels glisten,
   Greener than emeralds shining in the sun.
Whence comes the magic? Listen, sweetheart, listen!
   The mocking-bird is singing: Spring is begun.

SONGS OUT OF DOORS

Hark, in his song no tremor of misgiving!
    All of his heart he pours into his lay,—
"Love, love, love, and pure delight of living:
    Winter is forgotten: here's a happy day!"
Fair in your face I read the flowery presage,
    Snowy on your brow and rosy on your mouth:
Sweet in your voice I hear the season's message,—
    Love, love, love, and Spring in the South!

1904.

A NOON SONG

There are songs for the morning and songs for the night,
  For sunrise and sunset, the stars and the moon;
But who will give praise to the fulness of light,
  And sing us a song of the glory of noon?
    Oh, the high noon, the clear noon,
      The noon with golden crest;
      When the blue sky burns, and the great sun turns
      With his face to the way of the west!

How swiftly he rose in the dawn of his strength!
  How slowly he crept as the morning wore by!
Ah, steep was the climbing that led him at length
  To the height of his throne in the wide summer sky.
    Oh, the long toil, the slow toil,
      The toil that may not rest,
      Till the sun looks down from his journey's crown,
      To the wonderful way of the west!

Then a quietness falls over meadow and hill,
  The wings of the wind in the forest are furled,
The river runs softly, the birds are all still,
  The workers are resting all over the world.
    Oh, the good hour, the kind hour,
      The hour that calms the breast!
      Little inn half-way on the road of the day,
      Where it follows the turn to the west!

SONGS OUT OF DOORS

There's a plentiful feast in the maple-tree shade,
  The lilt of a song to an old-fashioned tune,
The talk of a friend, or the kiss of a maid,
  To sweeten the cup that we drink to the noon.
     Oh, the deep noon, the full noon,
      Of all the day the best!
     When the blue sky burns, and the great sun turns
      To his home by the way of the west!

1906.

LIGHT BETWEEN THE TREES

Long, long, long the trail
   Through the brooding forest-gloom,
Down the shadowy, lonely vale
   Into silence, like a room
     Where the light of life has fled,
   And the jealous curtains close
   Round the passionless repose
     Of the silent dead.

Plod, plod, plod away,
   Step by step in mouldering moss;
Thick branches bar the day
   Over languid streams that cross
     Softly, slowly, with a sound
   Like a smothered weeping,
   In their aimless creeping
     Through enchanted ground.

"Yield, yield, yield thy quest,"
   Whispers through the woodland deep;
"Come to me and be at rest;
   I am slumber, I am sleep."
     Then the weary feet would fail,
   But the never-daunted will
   Urges "Forward, forward still!
     Press along the trail!"

SONGS OUT OF DOORS

Breast, breast, breast the slope
  See, the path is growing steep.
Hark! a little song of hope
  Where the stream begins to leap.
    Though the forest, far and wide,
  Still shuts out the bending blue,
  We shall finally win through,
    Cross the long divide.

On, on, on we tramp!
  Will the journey never end?
Over yonder lies the camp;
  Welcome waits us there, my friend.
    Can we reach it ere the night?
  Upward, upward, never fear!
  Look, the summit must be near;
    See the line of light!

Red, red, red the shine
  Of the splendour in the west,
Glowing through the ranks of pine,
  Clear along the mountain-crest!
  Long, long, long the trail
  Out of sorrow's lonely vale;
    But at last the traveller sees
    Light between the trees!

March, 1904.

THE HERMIT THRUSH

O WONDERFUL! How liquid clear
The molten gold of that ethereal tone,
Floating and falling through the wood alone,
A hermit-hymn poured out for God to hear!

O holy, holy, holy! Hyaline,
Long light, low light, glory of eventide!
Love far away, far up,—up,—love divine!
Little love, too, for ever, ever near,
Warm love, earth love, tender love of mine,
In the leafy dark where you hide,
You are mine,—mine,—mine!

Ah, my belovèd, do you feel with me
The hidden virtue of that melody,
The rapture and the purity of love,
The heavenly joy that can not find the word?
Then, while we wait again to hear the bird,
Come very near to me, and do not move,—
Now, hermit of the woodland, fill anew
The cool, green cup of air with harmony,
And we will drink the wine of love with you.

May, 1908.

TURN O' THE TIDE

The tide flows in to the harbour,—
  The bold tide, the gold tide, the flood o' the sunlit sea,—
And the little ships riding at anchor,
  Are swinging and slanting their prows to the ocean, panting
    To lift their wings to the wide wild air,
    And venture a voyage they know not where,—
To fly away and be free!

The tide runs out of the harbour,—
  The low tide, the slow tide, the ebb o' the moonlit bay,—
And the little ships rocking at anchor,
  Are rounding and turning their bows to the landward, yearning
    To breathe the breath of the sun-warmed strand,
    To rest in the lee of the high hill land,—
To hold their haven and stay!

My heart goes round with the vessels,—
  My wild heart, my child heart, in love with the sea and the land,—
And the turn o' the tide passes through it,
  In rising and falling with mystical currents, calling
    At morn, to range where the far waves foam,
    At night, to a harbour in love's true home,
  With the hearts that understand!

Seal Harbour, August 12, 1911.

SIERRA MADRE

O MOTHER mountains! billowing far to the snow-lands,
   Robed in aërial amethyst, silver, and blue,
Why do ye look so proudly down on the lowlands?
   What have their groves and gardens to do with you?

Theirs is the languorous charm of the orange and myrtle,
   Theirs are the fruitage and fragrance of Eden of old,—
Broad-boughed oaks in the meadows fair and fertile,
   Dark-leaved orchards gleaming with globes of gold.

You, in your solitude standing, lofty and lonely,
   Bear neither garden nor grove on your barren breasts;
Rough is the rock-loving growth of your canyons, and
     only
   Storm-battered pines and fir-trees cling to your crests.

Why are ye throned so high, and arrayed in splendour
   Richer than all the fields at your feet can claim?
What is your right, ye rugged peaks, to the tender
   Queenly promise and pride of the mother-name?

Answered the mountains, dim in the distance dreaming:
   "Ours are the forests that treasure the riches of rain;
Ours are the secret springs and the rivulets gleaming
   Silverly down through the manifold bloom of the plain.

SONGS OUT OF DOORS

"Vain were the toiling of men in the dust of the dry
    land,
Vain were the ploughing and planting in waterless fields,
Save for the life-giving currents we send from the sky-
    land,
Save for the fruit our embrace with the storm-cloud
    yields."

O mother mountains, Madre Sierra, I love you!
    Rightly you reign o'er the vale that your bounty
        fills,—
Kissed by the sun, or with big, bright stars above you,—
    I murmur your name and lift up mine eyes to the hills.

Pasadena, March, 1913.

THE GRAND CANYON
DAYBREAK

WHAT makes the lingering Night so cling to thee?
Thou vast, profound, primeval hiding-place
Of ancient secrets,—gray and ghostly gulf
Cleft in the green of this high forest land,
And crowded in the dark with giant forms!
Art thou a grave, a prison, or a shrine?

A stillness deeper than the dearth of sound
Broods over thee: a living silence breathes
Perpetual incense from thy dim abyss.
The morning-stars that sang above the bower
Of Eden, passing over thee, are dumb
With trembling bright amazement; and the Dawn
Steals through the glimmering pines with naked feet,
Her hand upon her lips, to look on thee!
She peers into thy depths with silent prayer
For light, more light, to part thy purple veil.
O Earth, swift-rolling Earth, reveal, reveal,—
Turn to the East, and show upon thy breast
The mightiest marvel in the realm of Time!

SONGS OUT OF DOORS

'Tis done,—the morning miracle of light,—
The resurrection of the world of hues
That die with dark, and daily rise again
With every rising of the splendid Sun!

Be still, my heart! Now Nature holds her breath
To see the solar flood of radiance leap
Across the chasm, and crown the western rim
Of alabaster with a far-away
Rampart of pearl, and flowing down by walls
Of changeful opal, deepen into gold
Of topaz, rosy gold of tourmaline,
Crimson of garnet, green and gray of jade,
Purple of amethyst, and ruby red,
Beryl, and sard, and royal porphyry;
Until the cataract of colour breaks
Upon the blackness of the granite floor.

How far below! And all between is cleft
And carved into a hundred curving miles
Of unimagined architecture! Tombs,
Temples, and colonnades are neighboured there
By fortresses that Titans might defend,
And amphitheatres where Gods might strive.
Cathedrals, buttressed with unnumbered tiers
Of ruddy rock, lift to the sapphire sky
A single spire of marble pure as snow;
And huge aërial palaces arise

THE GRAND CANYON

Like mountains built of unconsuming flame.
Along the weathered walls, or standing deep
In riven valleys where no foot may tread,
Are lonely pillars, and tall monuments
Of perished æons and forgotten things.
My sight is baffled by the wide array
Of countless forms: my vision reels and swims
Above them, like a bird in whirling winds.
Yet no confusion fills the awful chasm;
But spacious order and a sense of peace
Brood over all. For every shape that looms
Majestic in the throng, is set apart
From all the others by its far-flung shade,
Blue, blue, as if a mountain-lake were there.

How still it is! Dear God, I hardly dare
To breathe, for fear the fathomless abyss
Will draw me down into eternal sleep.

What force has formed this masterpiece of awe?
What hands have wrought these wonders in the waste?
O river, gleaming in the narrow rift
Of gloom that cleaves the valley's nether deep,—
Fierce Colorado, prisoned by thy toil,
And blindly toiling still to reach the sea,—
Thy waters, gathered from the snows and springs
Amid the Utah hills, have carved this road
Of glory to the Californian Gulf.

SONGS OUT OF DOORS

But now, O sunken stream, thy splendour lost,
'Twixt iron walls thou rollest turbid waves,
Too far away to make their fury heard!

At sight of thee, thou sullen labouring slave
Of gravitation,—yellow torrent poured
From distant mountains by no will of thine,
Through thrice a hundred centuries of slow
Fallings and liftings of the crust of Earth,—
At sight of thee my spirit sinks and fails.
Art thou alone the Maker? Is the blind
Unconscious power that drew thee dumbly down
To cut this gash across the layered globe,
The sole creative cause of all I see?
Are force and matter all? The rest a dream?

Then is thy gorge a canyon of despair,
A prison for the soul of man, a grave
Of all his dearest daring hopes! The world
Wherein we live and move is meaningless,
No spirit here to answer to our own!
The stars without a guide: The chance-born Earth
Adrift in space, no Captain on the ship:
Nothing in all the universe to prove
Eternal wisdom and eternal love!
And man, the latest accident of Time,—
Who thinks he loves, and longs to understand,
Who vainly suffers, and in vain is brave,

THE GRAND CANYON

Who dupes his heart with immortality,—
Man is a living lie,—a bitter jest
Upon himself,—a conscious grain of sand
Lost in a desert of unconsciousness,
Thirsting for God and mocked by his own thirst.

Spirit of Beauty, mother of delight,
Thou fairest offspring of Omnipotence
Inhabiting this lofty lone abode,
Speak to my heart again and set me free
From all these doubts that darken earth and heaven!
Who sent thee forth into the wilderness
To bless and comfort all who see thy face?
Who clad thee in this more than royal robe
Of rainbows? Who designed these jewelled thrones
For thee, and wrought these glittering palaces?
Who gave thee power upon the soul of man
To lift him up through wonder into joy?
God! let the radiant cliffs bear witness, God!
Let all the shining pillars signal, God!
He only, on the mystic loom of light,
Hath woven webs of loveliness to clothe
His most majestic works: and He alone
Hath delicately wrought the cactus-flower
To star the desert floor with rosy bloom.

SONGS OUT OF DOORS

O Beauty, handiwork of the Most High,
Where'er thou art He tells his Love to man,
And lo, the day breaks, and the shadows flee!

Now, far beyond all language and all art
In thy wild splendour, Canyon marvellous,
The secret of thy stillness lies unveiled
In wordless worship! This is holy ground;
Thou art no grave, no prison, but a shrine.
Garden of Temples filled with Silent Praise,
If God were blind thy Beauty could not be!

February 24-26, 1913.

THE HEAVENLY HILLS OF HOLLAND

The heavenly hills of Holland,—
　How wondrously they rise
Above the smooth green pastures
　Into the azure skies!
With blue and purple hollows,
　With peaks of dazzling snow,
Along the far horizon
　The clouds are marching slow.

No mortal foot has trodden
　The summits of that range,
Nor walked those mystic valleys
　Whose colours ever change;
Yet we possess their beauty,
　And visit them in dreams,
While ruddy gold of sunset
　From cliff and canyon gleams.

In days of cloudless weather
　They melt into the light;
When fog and mist surround us
　They're hidden from our sight;
But when returns a season
　Clear shining after rain,
While the northwest wind is blowing,
　We see the hills again.

SONGS OUT OF DOORS

The old Dutch painters loved them,
  Their pictures show them fair,—
Old Hobbema and Ruysdael,
  Van Goyen and Vermeer.
Above the level landscape,
  Rich polders, long-armed mills,
Canals and ancient cities,—
  Float Holland's heavenly hills.

The Hague, November, 1916.

FLOOD-TIDE OF FLOWERS

IN HOLLAND

The laggard winter ebbed so slow
With freezing rain and melting snow,
It seemed as if the earth would stay
Forever where the tide was low,
In sodden green and watery gray.

But now from depths beyond our sight,
The tide is turning in the night,
And floods of colour long concealed
Come silent rising toward the light,
Through garden bare and empty field.

And first, along the sheltered nooks,
The crocus runs in little brooks
Of joyance, till by light made bold
They show the gladness of their looks
In shining pools of white and gold.

The tiny scilla, sapphire blue,
Is gently seeping in, to strew
The earth with heaven; and sudden rills
Of sunlit yellow, sweeping through,
Spread into lakes of daffodils.

SONGS OUT OF DOORS

The hyacinths, with fragrant heads,
Have overflowed their sandy beds,
And fill the earth with faint perfume,
The breath that Spring around her sheds.
And now the tulips break in bloom!

A sea, a rainbow-tinted sea,
A splendour and a mystery,
Floods o'er the fields of faded gray:
The roads are full of folks in glee,
For lo,—to-day is Easter Day!

April, 1916.

ODE

GOD OF THE OPEN AIR

I

Thou who hast made thy dwelling fair
  With flowers below, above with starry lights
And set thine altars everywhere,—
    On mountain heights,
In woodlands dim with many a dream,
    In valleys bright with springs,
And on the curving capes of every stream:
Thou who hast taken to thyself the wings
    Of morning, to abide
Upon the secret places of the sea,
  And on far islands, where the tide
Visits the beauty of untrodden shores,
Waiting for worshippers to come to thee
    In thy great out-of-doors!
To thee I turn, to thee I make my prayer,
    God of the open air.

II

Seeking for thee, the heart of man
    Lonely and longing ran,
In that first, solitary hour,
    When the mysterious power

SONGS OUT OF DOORS

To know and love the wonder of the morn
Was breathed within him, and his soul was born;
    And thou didst meet thy child,
    Not in some hidden shrine,
But in the freedom of the garden wild,
    And take his hand in thine,—
There all day long in Paradise he walked,
And in the cool of evening with thee talked.

III

Lost, long ago, that garden bright and pure,
Lost, that calm day too perfect to endure,
And lost the child-like love that worshipped and was
    sure!
For men have dulled their eyes with sin,
And dimmed the light of heaven with doubt,
And built their temple walls to shut thee in,
And framed their iron creeds to shut thee out.
    But not for thee the closing of the door,
        O Spirit unconfined!
        Thy ways are free
        As is the wandering wind,
And thou hast wooed thy children, to restore
    Their fellowship with thee,
In peace of soul and simpleness of mind.

GOD OF THE OPEN AIR

IV

Joyful the heart that, when the flood rolled by,
Leaped up to see the rainbow in the sky;
And glad the pilgrim, in the lonely night,
For whom the hills of Haran, tier on tier,
Built up a secret stairway to the height
Where stars like angel eyes were shining clear.
From mountain-peaks, in many a land and age,
   Disciples of the Persian seer
Have hailed the rising sun and worshipped thee;
And wayworn followers of the Indian sage
Have found the peace of God beneath a spreading tree.

V

But One, but One,—ah, Son most dear,
And perfect image of the Love Unseen,—
   Walked every day in pastures green,
And all his life the quiet waters by,
Reading their beauty with a tranquil eye.
To him the desert was a place prepared
     For weary hearts to rest;
   The hillside was a temple blest;
   The grassy vale a banquet-room
Where he could feed and comfort many a guest.
     With him the lily shared
The vital joy that breathes itself in bloom;

SONGS OUT OF DOORS

And every bird that sang beside the nest
Told of the love that broods o'er every living thing.
    He watched the shepherd bring
His flock at sundown to the welcome fold,
    The fisherman at daybreak fling
His net across the waters gray and cold,
And all day long the patient reaper swing
His curving sickle through the harvest-gold.
So through the world the foot-path way he trod,
Breathing the air of heaven in every breath;
And in the evening sacrifice of death
Beneath the open sky he gave his soul to God.
Him will I trust, and for my Master take;
Him will I follow; and for his dear sake,
    God of the open air,
    To thee I make my prayer.

VI

From the prison of anxious thought that greed has builded,
From the fetters that envy has wrought and pride has gilded,
From the noise of the crowded ways and the fierce confusion,
From the folly that wastes its days in a world of illusion,
(Ah, but the life is lost that frets and languishes there!)
I would escape and be free in the joy of the open air.

GOD OF THE OPEN AIR

By the breadth of the blue that shines in silence o'er me,
By the length of the mountain-lines that stretch before
  me,
By the height of the cloud that sails, with rest in
  motion,
Over the plains and the vales to the measureless ocean,
(Oh, how the sight of the greater things enlarges the
  eyes!)
Draw me away from myself to the peace of the hills and
  skies.

While the tremulous leafy haze on the woodland is
  spreading,
And the bloom on the meadow betrays where May has
  been treading;
While the birds on the branches above, and the brooks
  flowing under,
Are singing together of love in a world full of wonder,
(Lo, in the magic of Springtime, dreams are changed
  into truth!)
Quicken my heart, and restore the beautiful hopes of
  youth.

By the faith that the wild-flowers show when they bloom
  unbidden,
By the calm of the river's flow to a goal that is hidden,
By the strength of the tree that clings to its deep founda-
  tion,

SONGS OUT OF DOORS

By the courage of birds' light wings on the long migration,
(Wonderful spirit of trust that abides in Nature's breast!)
Teach me how to confide, and live my life, and rest.

For the comforting warmth of the sun that my body embraces,
For the cool of the waters that run through the shadowy places,
For the balm of the breezes that brush my face with their fingers,
For the vesper-hymn of the thrush when the twilight lingers,
For the long breath, the deep breath, the breath of a heart without care,—
I will give thanks and adore thee, God of the open air!

VII

These are the gifts I ask
Of thee, Spirit serene:
Strength for the daily task,
Courage to face the road,
Good cheer to help me bear the traveller's load,
And, for the hours of rest that come between,
An inward joy in all things heard and seen.

GOD OF THE OPEN AIR

    These are the sins I fain
    Would have thee take away:
    Malice, and cold disdain,
    Hot anger, sullen hate,
Scorn of the lowly, envy of the great,
And discontent that casts a shadow gray
On all the brightness of the common day.
    These are the things I prize
    And hold of dearest worth:
    Light of the sapphire skies,
    Peace of the silent hills,
Shelter of forests, comfort of the grass,
Music of birds, murmur of little rills,
Shadows of cloud that swiftly pass,
    And, after showers,
    The smell of flowers
    And of the good brown earth,—
And best of all, along the way, friendship and mirth.
    So let me keep
    These treasures of the humble heart
    In true possession, owning them by love;
    And when at last I can no longer move
    Among them freely, but must part
From the green fields and from the waters clear,
    Let me not creep
Into some darkened room and hide
From all that makes the world so bright and dear;
    But throw the windows wide

SONGS OUT OF DOORS

    To welcome in the light;
And while I clasp a well-belovèd hand,
    Let me once more have sight
Of the deep sky and the far-smiling land,—
    Then gently fall on sleep,
And breathe my body back to Nature's care,
My spirit out to thee, God of the open air.

1904.

NARRATIVE POEMS

THE TOILING OF FELIX
A LEGEND ON A NEW SAYING OF JESUS

In the rubbish heaps of the ancient city of Oxyrhynchus, near the River Nile, a party of English explorers, in the winter of 1897, discovered a fragment of a papyrus book, written in the second or third century, and hitherto unknown. This single leaf contained parts of seven short sentences of Christ, each introduced by the words, "Jesus says." It is to the fifth of these Sayings of Jesus that the following poem refers.

THE TOILING OF FELIX

I

PRELUDE

Hear a word that Jesus spake
  Nineteen hundred years ago,
  Where the crimson lilies blow
Round the blue Tiberian lake:
There the bread of life He brake,
  Through the fields of harvest walking
  With His lowly comrades, talking
  Of the secret thoughts that feed
  Weary souls in time of need.
Art thou hungry? Come and take;
Hear the word that Jesus spake!
'Tis the sacrament of labour, bread and wine divinely blest;
Friendship's food and sweet refreshment, strength and courage, joy and rest.

  But this word the Master said
    Long ago and far away,
    Silent and forgotten lay
  Buried with the silent dead,
  Where the sands of Egypt spread
    Sea-like, tawny billows heaping
    Over ancient cities sleeping,

NARRATIVE POEMS

While the River Nile between
Rolls its summer flood of green
Rolls its autumn flood of red:
There the word the Master said,
Written on a frail papyrus, wrinkled, scorched by fire, and torn,
Hidden by God's hand was waiting for its resurrection morn.

Now at last the buried word
By the delving spade is found,
Sleeping in the quiet ground.
Now the call of life is heard:
Rise again, and like a bird,
Fly abroad on wings of gladness
Through the darkness and the sadness,
Of the toiling age, and sing
Sweeter than the voice of Spring,
Till the hearts of men are stirred
By the music of the word,—
Gospel for the heavy-laden, answer to the labourer's cry:
"Raise the stone, and thou shalt find me; cleave the wood and there am I."

THE TOILING OF FELIX

II

LEGEND

Brother-men who look for Jesus, long to see Him close and clear,
Hearken to the tale of Felix, how he found the Master near.

Born in Egypt, 'neath the shadow of the crumbling gods of night,
He forsook the ancient darkness, turned his young heart toward the Light.

Seeking Christ, in vain he waited for the vision of the Lord;
Vainly pondered many volumes where the creeds of men were stored;

Vainly shut himself in silence, keeping vigil night and day;
Vainly haunted shrines and churches where the Christians came to pray.

One by one he dropped the duties of the common life of care,
Broke the human ties that bound him, laid his spirit waste and bare,

NARRATIVE POEMS

Hoping that the Lord would enter that deserted dwelling-
    place,
And reward the loss of all things with the vision of His
    face.

Still the blessed vision tarried; still the light was unre-
    vealed;
Still the Master, dim and distant, kept His countenance
    concealed.

Fainter grew the hope of finding, wearier grew the fruit-
    less quest;
Prayer and penitence and fasting gave no comfort, brought
    no rest.

Lingering in the darkened temple, ere the lamp of faith
    went out,
Felix knelt before the altar, lonely, sad, and full of
    doubt.

"Hear me, O my Lord and Master," from the altar-step
    he cried,
"Let my one desire be granted, let my hope be satisfied!

"Only once I long to see Thee, in the fulness of Thy
    grace:
Break the clouds that now enfold Thee, with the sunrise
    of Thy face!

THE TOILING OF FELIX

"All that men desire and treasure have I counted loss for Thee;
Every hope have I forsaken, save this one, my Lord to see.

"Loosed the sacred bands of friendship, solitary stands my heart;
Thou shalt be my sole companion when I see Thee as Thou art.

"From Thy distant throne in glory, flash upon my inward sight,
Fill the midnight of my spirit with the splendour of Thy light.

"All Thine other gifts and blessings, common mercies, I disown;
Separated from my brothers, I would see Thy face alone.

"I have watched and I have waited as one waiteth for the morn:
Still the veil is never lifted, still Thou leavest me forlorn.

"Now I seek Thee in the desert, where the holy hermits dwell;
There, beside the saint Serapion, I will find a lonely cell.

NARRATIVE POEMS

"There at last Thou wilt be gracious; there Thy presence, long-concealed,
In the solitude and silence to my heart shall be revealed.

"Thou wilt come, at dawn or twilight, o'er the rolling waves of sand;
I shall see Thee close beside me, I shall touch Thy pierced hand.

"Lo, Thy pilgrim kneels before Thee; bless my journey with a word;
Tell me now that if I follow, I shall find Thee, O my Lord!"

Felix listened: through the darkness, like a murmur of the wind,
Came a gentle sound of stillness: "Never faint, and thou shalt find."

Long and toilsome was his journey through the heavy land of heat,
Egypt's blazing sun above him, blistering sand beneath his feet.

Patiently he plodded onward, from the pathway never erred,
Till he reached the river-headland called the Mountain of the Bird.

THE TOILING OF FELIX

There the tribes of air assemble, once a year, their noisy flock,
Then, departing, leave a sentinel perched upon the highest rock.

Far away, on joyful pinions, over land and sea they fly;
But the watcher on the summit lonely stands against the sky.

There the eremite Serapion in a cave had made his bed;
There the faithful bands of pilgrims sought his blessing, brought him bread.

Month by month, in deep seclusion, hidden in the rocky cleft,
Dwelt the hermit, fasting, praying; once a year the cave he left.

On that day a happy pilgrim, chosen out of all the band,
Won a special sign of favour from the holy hermit's hand.

Underneath the narrow window, at the doorway closely sealed,
While the afterglow of sunset deepened round him, Felix kneeled.

NARRATIVE POEMS

"Man of God, of men most holy, thou whose gifts cannot
    be priced!
Grant me thy most precious guerdon; tell me how to
    find the Christ."

Breathless, Felix bent and listened, but no answering
    voice he heard;
Darkness folded, dumb and deathlike, round the Mountain of the Bird.

Then he said, "The saint is silent; he would teach my
    soul to wait:
I will tarry here in patience, like a beggar at his gate."

Near the dwelling of the hermit Felix found a rude
    abode,
In a shallow tomb deserted, close beside the pilgrim-road.

So the faithful pilgrims saw him waiting there without
    complaint,—
Soon they learned to call him holy, fed him as they fed
    the saint.

Day by day he watched the sunrise flood the distant plain
    with gold,
While the River Nile beneath him, silvery coiling, seaward rolled.

THE TOILING OF FELIX

Night by night he saw the planets range their glittering court on high,
Saw the moon, with queenly motion, mount her throne and rule the sky.

Morn advanced and midnight fled, in visionary pomp attired;
Never morn and never midnight brought the vision long-desired.

Now at last the day is dawning when Serapion makes his gift;
Felix kneels before the threshold, hardly dares his eyes to lift.

Now the cavern door uncloses, now the saint above him stands,
Blesses him without a word, and leaves a token in his hands.

'Tis the guerdon of thy waiting! Look, thou happy pilgrim, look!
Nothing but a tattered fragment of an old papyrus book.

Read! perchance the clue to guide thee hidden in the words may lie:
"*Raise the stone, and thou shalt find me; cleave the wood, and there am I.*"

NARRATIVE POEMS

Can it be the mighty Master spake such simple words as these?
Can it be that men must seek Him at their toil 'mid rocks and trees?

Disappointed, heavy-hearted, from the Mountain of the Bird
Felix mournfully descended, questioning the Master's word.

Not for him a sacred dwelling, far above the haunts of men:
He must turn his footsteps backward to the common life again.

From a quarry near the river, hollowed out amid the hills,
Rose the clattering voice of labour, clanking hammers, clinking drills.

Dust, and noise, and hot confusion made a Babel of the spot:
There, among the lowliest workers, Felix sought and found his lot.

Now he swung the ponderous mallet, smote the iron in the rock—
Muscles quivering, tingling, throbbing—blow on blow and shock on shock;

THE TOILING OF FELIX

Now he drove the willow wedges, wet them till they swelled and split,
With their silent strength, the fragment, sent it thundering down the pit.

Now the groaning tackle raised it; now the rollers made it slide;
Harnessed men, like beasts of burden, drew it to the river-side.

Now the palm-trees must be riven, massive timbers hewn and dressed;
Rafts to bear the stones in safety on the rushing river's breast.

Axe and auger, saw and chisel, wrought the will of man in wood:
'Mid the many-handed labour Felix toiled, and found it good.

Every day the blood ran fleeter through his limbs and round his heart;
Every night he slept the sweeter, knowing he had done his part.

Dreams of solitary saintship faded from him; but, instead,
Came a sense of daily comfort in the toil for daily bread.

NARRATIVE POEMS

Far away, across the river, gleamed the white walls of
 the town
Whither all the stones and timbers day by day were
 floated down.

There the workman saw his labour taking form and bear-
 ing fruit,
Like a tree with splendid branches rising from a humble
 root.

Looking at the distant city, temples, houses, domes, and
 towers,
Felix cried in exultation: "All that mighty work is
 ours.

"Every toiler in the quarry, every builder on the shore,
Every chopper in the palm-grove, every raftsman at the
 oar,

"Hewing wood and drawing water, splitting stones and
 cleaving sod,
All the dusty ranks of labour, in the regiment of
 God,

"March together toward His triumph, do the task His
 hands prepare:
Honest toil is holy service; faithful work is praise and
 prayer."

THE TOILING OF FELIX

While he bore the heat and burden Felix felt the sense of rest
Flowing softly like a fountain, deep within his weary breast;

Felt the brotherhood of labour, rising round him like a tide,
Overflow his heart and join him to the workers at his side.

Oft he cheered them with his singing at the breaking of the light,
Told them tales of Christ at noonday, taught them words of prayer at night.

Once he bent above a comrade fainting in the mid-day heat,
Sheltered him with woven palm-leaves, gave him water, cool and sweet.

Then it seemed, for one swift moment, secret radiance filled the place;
Underneath the green palm-branches flashed a look of Jesus' face.

Once again, a raftsman, slipping, plunged beneath the stream and sank;
Swiftly Felix leaped to rescue, caught him, drew him toward the bank—

NARRATIVE POEMS

Battling with the cruel river, using all his strength to save—
Did he dream? or was there One beside him walking on the wave?

Now at last the work was ended, grove deserted, quarry stilled;
Felix journeyed to the city that his hands had helped to build.

In the darkness of the temple, at the closing hour of day,
As of old he sought the altar, as of old he knelt to pray:

"Hear me, O Thou hidden Master! Thou hast sent a word to me;
It is written—Thy commandment—I have kept it faithfully.

"Thou hast bid me leave the visions of the solitary life,
Bear my part in human labour, take my share in human strife.

"I have done Thy bidding, Master; raised the rock and felled the tree,
Swung the axe and plied the hammer, working every day for Thee.

THE TOILING OF FELIX

"Once it seemed I saw Thy presence through the bending
   palm-leaves gleam;
Once upon the flowing water— Nay, I know not; 'twas
   a dream!

"This I know: Thou hast been near me: more than this
   I dare not ask.
Though I see Thee not, I love Thee. Let me do Thy
   humblest task!"

Through the dimness of the temple slowly dawned a
   mystic light;
There the Master stood in glory, manifest to mortal
   sight:

Hands that bore the mark of labour, brow that bore the
   print of care;
Hands of power, divinely tender; brow of light, divinely
   fair.

"Hearken, good and faithful servant, true disciple, loyal
   friend!
Thou hast followed me and found me; I will keep thee
   to the end.

"Well I know thy toil and trouble; often weary, fainting,
   worn,
I have lived the life of labour, heavy burdens I have borne.

NARRATIVE POEMS

"Never in a prince's palace have I slept on golden bed,
Never in a hermit's cavern have I eaten unearned bread.

"Born within a lowly stable, where the cattle round me stood,
Trained a carpenter in Nazareth, I have toiled, and found it good.

"They who tread the path of labour follow where my feet have trod;
They who work without complaining do the holy will of God.

"Where the many toil together, there am I among my own;
Where the tired workman sleepeth, there am I with him alone.

"I, the peace that passeth knowledge, dwell amid the daily strife;
I, the bread of heaven, am broken in the sacrament of life.

"Every task, however simple, sets the soul that does it free;
Every deed of love and mercy, done to man, is done to me.

THE TOILING OF FELIX

"Thou hast learned the open secret; thou hast come to me for rest;
With thy burden, in thy labour, thou art Felix, doubly blest.

"Nevermore thou needest seek me; I am with thee everywhere;
Raise the stone, and thou shalt find me; cleave the wood, and I am there."

III

ENVOY

The legend of Felix is ended, the toiling of Felix is done;
The Master has paid him his wages, the goal of his journey is won;
He rests, but he never is idle; a thousand years pass like a day,
In the glad surprise of that Paradise where work is sweeter than play.

Yet often the King of that country comes out from His tireless host,
And walks in this world of the weary as if He loved it the most;
For here in the dusty confusion, with eyes that are heavy and dim,
He meets again the labouring men who are looking and longing for Him.

NARRATIVE POEMS

He cancels the curse of Eden, and brings them a blessing
    instead:
Blessed are they that labour, for Jesus partakes of their
    bread.
He puts His hand to their burdens, He enters their homes
    at night:
Who does his best shall have as a guest the Master of
    life and light.

And courage will come with His presence, and patience
    return at His touch,
And manifold sins be forgiven to those who love Him
    much;
The cries of envy and anger will change to the songs of
    cheer,
The toiling age will forget its rage when the Prince of
    Peace draws near.

This is the gospel of labour, ring it, ye bells of the kirk!
The Lord of Love came down from above, to live with
    the men who work.
This is the rose that He planted, here in the thorn-curst
    soil:
Heaven is blest with perfect rest, but the blessing of
    Earth is toil.

1898.

VERA

I

A SILENT world,—yet full of vital joy
Uttered in rhythmic movements manifold,
And sunbeams flashing on the face of things
Like sudden smilings of divine delight,—
A world of many sorrows too, revealed
In fading flowers and withering leaves and dark
Tear-laden clouds, and tearless, clinging mists
That hung above the earth too sad to weep,—
A world of fluent change, and changeless flow,
And infinite suggestion of new thought,
Reflected in the crystal of the heart,—
A world of many meanings but no words,
A silent world was Vera's home.
                                        For her
The inner doors of sound were closely sealed
The outer portals, delicate as shells
Suffused with faintest rose of far-off morn,
Like underglow of daybreak in the sea,—
The ear-gates of the garden of her soul,
Shaded by drooping tendrils of brown hair,—
Waited in vain for messengers to pass,
And thread the labyrinth with flying feet,
And swiftly knock upon the inmost door,
And enter in, and speak the mystic word.

NARRATIVE POEMS

But through those gates no message ever came.
Only with eyes did she behold and see,—
With eyes as luminous and bright and brown
As waters of a woodland river,—eyes
That questioned so they almost seemed to speak,
And answered so they almost seemed to hear,—
Only with wondering eyes did she behold
The silent splendour of a living world.

She saw the great wind ranging freely down
Interminable archways of the wood,
While tossing boughs and bending tree-tops hailed
His coming: but no sea-toned voice of pines,
No roaring of the oaks, no silvery song
Of poplars or of birches, followed him.
He passed; they waved their arms and clapped their hands;
There was no sound. The torrents from the hills
Leaped down their rocky pathways, like wild steeds
Breaking the yoke and shaking manes of foam.
The lowland brooks coiled smoothly through the fields,
And softly spread themselves in glistening lakes
Whose ripples merrily danced among the reeds.
The standing waves that ever keep their place
In the swift rapids, curled upon themselves,
And seemed about to break and never broke;
And all the wandering waves that fill the sea

VERA

Came buffeting in along the stony shore,
Or plunging in along the level sands,
Or creeping in along the winding creeks
And inlets. Yet from all the ceaseless flow
And turmoil of the restless element
Came neither song of joy nor sob of grief;
For there were many waters, but no voice.

Silent the actors all on Nature's stage
Performed their parts before her watchful eyes,
Coming and going, making war and love,
Working and playing, all without a sound.
The oxen drew their load with swaying necks;
The cows came sauntering home along the lane;
The nodding sheep were led from field to fold
In mute obedience. Down the woodland track
The hounds with panting sides and lolling tongues
Pursued their flying prey in noiseless haste.
The birds, the most alive of living things,
Mated, and built their nests, and reared their young,
And swam the flood of air like tiny ships
Rising and falling over unseen waves,
And, gathering in great navies, bore away
To North or South, without a note of song.

All these were Vera's playmates; and she loved
To watch them, wondering oftentimes how well
They knew their parts, and how the drama moved

NARRATIVE POEMS

So swiftly, smoothly on from scene to scene
Without confusion. But she sometimes dreamed
There must be something hidden in the play
Unknown to her, an utterance of life
More clear than action and more deep than looks.
And this she felt most deeply when she watched
Her human comrades and the throngs of men,
Who met and parted oft with moving lips
That had a meaning more than she could see.
She saw a lover bend above a maid,
With moving lips; and though he touched her not
A sudden rose of joy bloomed in her face.
She saw a hater stand before his foe
And move his lips; whereat the other shrank
As if he had been smitten on the mouth.
She saw the regiments of toiling men
Marshalled in ranks and led by moving lips.
And once she saw a sight more strange than all:
A crowd of people sitting charmed and still
Around a little company of men
Who touched their hands in measured, rhythmic time
To curious instruments; a woman stood
Among them, with bright eyes and heaving breast,
And lifted up her face and moved her lips.
Then Vera wondered at the idle play,
But when she looked around, she saw the glow
Of deep delight on every face, as if
Some visitor from a celestial world

VERA

Had brought glad tidings. But to her alone
No angel entered, for the choir of sound
Was vacant in the temple of her soul,
And ˙worship lacked her golden crown of song.

So when by vision baffled and perplexed
She saw that all the world could not be seen,
And knew she could not know the whole of life
Unless a hidden gate should be unsealed,
She felt imprisoned. In her heart there grew
The bitter creeping plant of discontent,
The plant that only grows in prison soil,
Whose root is hunger and whose fruit is pain.
The springs of still delight and tranquil joy
Were drained as dry as desert dust to feed
That never-flowering vine, whose tendrils clung
With strangling touch around the bloom of life
And made it wither. Vera could not rest
Within the limits of her silent world;
Along its dumb and desolate paths she roamed
A captive, looking sadly for escape.

Now in those distant days, and in that land
Remote, there lived a Master wonderful,
Who knew the secret of all life, and could,
With gentle touches and with potent words,
Open all gates that ever had been sealed,
And loose all prisoners whom Fate had bound.

NARRATIVE POEMS

Obscure he dwelt, not in the wilderness,
But in a hut among the throngs of men,
Concealed by meekness and simplicity.
And ever as he walked the city streets,
Or sat in quietude beside the sea,
Or trod the hillsides and the harvest fields,
The multitude passed by and knew him not.
But there were some who knew, and turned to him
For help; and unto all who asked, he gave.
Thus Vera came, and found him in the field,
And knew him by the pity in his face.
She knelt to him and held him by one hand,
And laid the other hand upon her lips
In mute entreaty. Then she lifted up
The coils of hair that hung about her neck,
And bared the beauty of the gates of sound,—
Those virgin gates through which no voice had passed,—
She made them bare before the Master's sight,
And looked into the kindness of his face
With eyes that spoke of all her prisoned pain,
And told her great desire without a word.

The Master waited long in silent thought,
As one reluctant to bestow a gift,
Not for the sake of holding back the thing
Entreated, but because he surely knew
Of something better that he fain would give
If only she would ask it. Then he stooped

VERA

To Vera, smiling, touched her ears and spoke:
"Open, fair gates, and you, reluctant doors,
Within the ivory labyrinth of the ear,
Let fall the bar of silence and unfold!
Enter, you voices of all living things,
Enter the garden sealed,—but softly, slowly,
Not with a noise confused and broken tumult,—
Come in an order sweet as I command you,
And bring the double gift of speech and hearing."

Vera began to hear. At first the wind
Breathed a low prelude of the birth of sound,
As if an organ far away were touched
By unseen fingers; then the little stream
That hurried down the hillside, swept the harp
Of music into merry, tinkling notes;
And then the lark that poised above her head
On wings a-quiver, overflowed the air
With showers of song; and one by one the tones
Of all things living, in an order sweet,
Without confusion and with deepening power,
Entered the garden sealed. And last of all
The Master's voice, the human voice divine,
Passed through the gates and called her by her name,
And Vera heard.

NARRATIVE POEMS

II

What rapture of new life
Must come to one for whom a silent world
Is suddenly made vocal, and whose heart
By the same magic is awaked at once,
Without the learner's toil and long delay,
Out of a night of dumbly moving dreams,
Into a day that overflows with music!
This joy was Vera's; and to her it seemed
As if a new creative morn had risen
Upon the earth, and after the full week
When living things unfolded silently,
And after the long, quiet Sabbath day,
When all was still, another day had dawned,
And through the calm expectancy of heaven
A secret voice had said, "Let all things speak."
The world responded with an instant joy;
And all the unseen avenues of sound
Were thronged with varying forms of viewless life.

To every living thing a voice was given
Distinct and personal. The forest trees
Were not more varied in their shades of green
Than in their tones of speech; and every bird
That nested in their branches had a song
Unknown to other birds and all his own.
The waters spoke a hundred dialects

VERA

Of one great language; now with pattering fall
Of raindrops on the glistening leaves, and now
With steady roar of rivers rushing down
To meet the sea, and now with rhythmic throb
And measured tumult of tempestuous waves,
And now with lingering lisp of creeping tides,—
The manifold discourse of many waters.
But most of all the human voice was full
Of infinite variety, and ranged
Along the scale of life's experience
With changing tones, and notes both sweet and sad,
All fitted to express some unseen thought,
Some vital motion of the hidden heart.
So Vera listened with her new-born sense
To all the messengers that passed the gates,
In measureless delight and utter trust,
Believing that they brought a true report
From every living thing of its true life,
And hoping that at last they would make clear
The mystery and the meaning of the world.

But soon there came a trouble in her joy,
A note discordant that dissolved the chord
And broke the bliss of hearing into pain.
Not from the harsher sounds and voices wild
Of anger and of anguish, that reveal
The secret strife in nature, and confess
The touch of sorrow on the heart of life,—

NARRATIVE POEMS

From these her trouble came not. For in these,
However sad, she felt the note of truth,
And truth, though sad, is always musical.
The raging of the tempest-ridden sea,
The crash of thunder, and the hollow moan
Of winds complaining round the mountain-crags,
The shrill and quavering cry of birds of prey,
The fiercer roar of conflict-loving beasts,—
All these wild sounds are potent in their place
Within life's mighty symphony; the charm
Of truth attunes them, and the hearing ear
Finds pleasure in their rude sincerity.
Even the broken and tumultuous noise
That rises from great cities, where the heart
Of human toil is beating heavily
With ceaseless murmurs of the labouring pulse,
Is not a discord; for it speaks to life
Of life unfeigned, and full of hopes and fears,
And touched through all the trouble of its notes
With something real and therefore glorious.

One voice alone of all that sound on earth,
Is hateful to the soul, and full of pain,—
The voice of falsehood. So when Vera heard
This mocking voice, and knew that it was false;
When first she learned that human lips can speak
The thing that is not, and betray the ear
Of simple trust with treachery of words;

VERA

The joy of hearing withered in her heart.
For now she felt that faithless messengers
Could pass the open and unguarded gates
Of sound, and bring a message all untrue,
Or half a truth that makes the deadliest lie,
Or idle babble, neither false nor true,
But hollow to the heart, and meaningless.
She heard the flattering voices of deceit,
That mask the hidden purposes of men
With fair attire of favourable words,
And hide the evil in the guise of good:
The voices vain and decorous and smooth,
That fill the world with empty-hearted talk;
The foolish voices, wandering and confused,
That never clearly speak the thing they would,
But ramble blindly round their true intent
And tangle sense in hopeless coils of sound,—
All these she heard, and with a deep mistrust
Began to doubt the value of her gift.
It seemed as if the world, the living world,
Sincere, and vast, and real, were still concealed,
And she, within the prison of her soul,
Still waiting silently to hear the voice
Of perfect knowledge and of perfect peace.

So with the burden of her discontent
She turned to seek the Master once again,
And found him sitting in the market-place,

NARRATIVE POEMS

Half-hidden in the shadow of a porch,
Alone among the careless crowd.
                              She spoke:
"Thy gift was great, dear Master, and my heart
Has thanked thee many times because I hear
But I have learned that hearing is not all;
For underneath the speech of men, there flows
Another current of their hidden thoughts;
Behind the mask of language I perceive
The eyes of things unsaid.
                       Touch me again,
O Master, with thy liberating hand,
And free me from the bondage of deceit.
Open another gate, and let me hear
The secret thoughts and purposes of men;
For only thus my heart will be at rest,
And only thus, at last, I shall perceive
The mystery and the meaning of the world."

The Master's face was turned aside from her;
His eyes looked far away, as if he saw
Something beyond her sight; and yet she knew
That he was listening; for her pleading voice
No sooner ceased than he put forth his hand
To touch her brow, and very gently spoke:
"Thou seekest for thyself a wondrous gift,—
The opening of the second gate, a gift
That many wise men have desired in vain:

VERA

But some have found it,—whether well or ill
For their own peace, they have attained the power
To hear unspoken thoughts of other men.
And thou hast begged this gift? Thou shalt receive,—
Not knowing what thou seekest,—it is thine:
The second gate is open! Thou shalt hear
All that men think and feel within their hearts:
Thy prayer is granted, daughter, go thy way!
But if thou findest sorrow on this path,
Come back again,—there is a path to peace."

III

Beyond our power of vision, poets say,
There is another world of forms unseen,
Yet visible to purer eyes than ours.
And if the crystal of our sight were clear,
We should behold the mountain-slopes of cloud,
The moving meadows of the untilled sea,
The groves of twilight and the dales of dawn,
And every wide and lonely field of air,
More populous than cities, crowded close
With living creatures of all shapes and hues.
But if that sight were ours, the things that now
Engage our eyes would seem but dull and dim
Beside the wonders of our new-found world,
And we should be amazed and overwhelmed
Not knowing how to use the plenitude
Of vision.

NARRATIVE POEMS

So in Vera's soul, at first,
The opening of the second gate of sound
Let in confusion like a whirling flood.
The murmur of a myriad-throated mob;
The trampling of an army through a place
Where echoes hide; the sudden, whistling flight
Of an innumerable flock of birds
Along the highway of the midnight sky;
The many-whispered rustling of the reeds
Beneath the passing feet of all the winds;
The long-drawn, inarticulate, wailing cry
Of million-pebbled beaches when the lash
Of stormy waves is drawn across their back,—
All these were less bewildering than to hear
What now she heard at once: the tangled sound
Of all that moves within the minds of men.
For now there was no measured flow of words
To mark the time; nor any interval
Of silence to repose the listening ear.
But through the dead of night, and through the calm
Of weary noon-tide, through the solemn hush
That fills the temple in the pause of praise,
And through the breathless awe in rooms of death,
She heard the ceaseless motion and the stir
Of never-silent hearts, that fill the world
With interwoven thoughts of good and ill,
With mingled music of delight and grief,
With songs of love, and bitter cries of hate,

VERA

With hymns of faith, and dirges of despair,
And murmurs deeper and more vague than all,—
Thoughts that are born and die without a name,
Or rather, never die, but haunt the soul,
With sad persistence, till a name is given.
These Vera heard, at first with mind perplexed
And half-benumbed by the disordered sound.
But soon a clearer sense began to pierce
The cloudy turmoil with discerning power.
She learned to know the tones of human thought
As plainly as she knew the tones of speech.
She could divide the evil from the good,
Interpreting the language of the mind,
And tracing every feeling like a thread
Within the mystic web the passions weave
From heart to heart around the living world.

But when at last the Master's second gift
Was perfected within her, and she heard
And understood the secret thoughts of men,
A sadness fell upon her, and the load
Of insupportable knowledge pressed her down
With weary wishes to know more, or less.
For all she knew was like a broken word
Inscribed upon the fragment of a ring;
And all she heard was like a broken strain
Preluding music that is never played.

NARRATIVE POEMS

Then she remembered in her sad unrest
The Master's parting word,—"a path to peace,"—
And turned again to seek him with her grief.
She found him in a hollow of the hills,
Beside a little spring that issued forth
Beneath the rocks and filled a mossy cup
With never-failing water. There he sat,
With waiting looks that welcomed her afar.
"I know that thou hast heard, my child," he said,
"For all the wonder of the world of sound
Is written in thy face. But hast thou heard,
Among the many voices, one of peace?
And is thy heart that hears the secret thoughts,
The hidden wishes and desires of men,
Content with hearing? Art thou satisfied?"
"Nay, Master," she replied, "thou knowest well
That I am not at rest, nor have I heard
The voice of perfect peace; but what I hear
Brings me disquiet and a troubled mind.
The evil voices in the souls of men,
Voices of rage and cruelty and fear
Have not dismayed me; for I have believed
The voices of the good, the kind, the true,
Are more in number and excel in strength.
There is more love than hate, more hope than fear,
In the deep throbbing of the human heart.
But while I listen to the troubled sound,
One thing torments me, and destroys my rest

VERA

And presses me with dull, unceasing pain.
For out of all the minds of all mankind,
There rises evermore a questioning voice
That asks the meaning of this mighty world
And finds no answer,—asks, and asks again,
With patient pleading or with wild complaint,
But wakens no response, except the sound
Of other questions, wandering to and fro,
From other souls in doubt. And so this voice
Persists above all others that I hear,
And binds them up together into one,
Until the mingled murmur of the world
Sounds through the inner temple of my heart
Like an eternal question, vainly asked
By every human soul that thinks and feels.
This is the heaviness that weighs me down,
And this the pain that will not let me rest.
Therefore, dear Master, shut the gates again,
And let me live in silence as before!
Or else,—and if there is indeed a gate
Unopened yet, through which I might receive
An answer in the voice of perfect peace—"

She ceased; and in her upward faltering tone
The question echoed.
              Then the Master said:
"There is another gate, not yet unclosed.
For through the outer portal of the ear

NARRATIVE POEMS

Only the outer voice of things may pass;
And through the middle doorway of the mind
Only the half-formed voice of human thoughts,
Uncertain and perplexed with endless doubt;
But through the inmost gate the spirit hears
The voice of that great Spirit who is Life.
Beneath the tones of living things He breathes
A deeper tone than ever ear hath heard;
And underneath the troubled thoughts of men
He thinks forever, and His thought is peace.
Behold, I touch thee once again, my child:
The third and last of those three hidden gates
That closed around thy soul and shut thee in,
Is open now, and thou shalt truly hear."

Then Vera heard. The spiritual gate
Was opened softly as a full-blown flower
Unfolds its heart to welcome in the dawn,
And on her listening face there shone a light
Of still amazement and completed joy
In the full gift of hearing.
                                    What she heard
I cannot tell; nor could she ever tell
In words; because all human words are vain.
There is no speech nor language, to express
The secret messages of God, that make
Perpetual music in the hearing heart.
Below the voice of waters, and above

EIGHT ECHOES FROM THE POEMS OF AUGUSTE ANGELLIER

I

THE IVORY CRADLE

The cradle I have made for thee
Is carved of orient ivory,
And curtained round with wavy silk
More white than hawthorn-bloom or milk.

A twig of box, a lilac spray,
Will drive the goblin-horde away;
And charm thy childlike heart to keep
Her happy dream and virgin sleep.

Within that pure and fragrant nest,
I'll rock thy gentle soul to rest,
With tender songs we need not fear
To have a passing angel hear.

Ah, long and long I fain would hold
The snowy curtain's guardian fold
Around thy crystal visions, born
In clearness of the early morn.

But look, the sun is glowing red
With triumph in his golden bed;

TWO SONGS OF HEINE

I

"EIN FICHTENBAUM"

A FIR-TREE standeth lonely
On a barren northern height,
Asleep, while winter covers
His rest with robes of white.

In dreams, he sees a palm-tree
In the golden morning-land;
She droops alone and silent
In burning wastes of sand.

II

"DU BIST WIE EINE BLUME"

Fair art thou as a flower
  And innocent and shy:
I look on thee and sorrow;
  I grieve, I know not why.

I long to lay, in blessing,
  My hand upon thy brow,
And pray that God may keep thee
  As fair and pure as now.

1872.

LOVE'S NEARNESS

I THINK of thee when golden sunbeams glimmer
    Across the sea;
And when the waves reflect the moon's pale shimmer
    I think of thee.

I see thy form when down the distant highway
    The dust-clouds rise;
In darkest night, above the mountain by-way
    I see thine eyes.

I hear thee when the ocean-tides returning
    Aloud rejoice;
And on the lonely moor in silence yearning
    I hear thy voice.

I dwell with thee; though thou art far removèd,
    Yet thou art near.
The sun goes down, the stars shine out,—Belovèd
    If thou wert here!

From the German of Goethe, 1898.

"RAPPELLE-TOI"

Remember, when the cool, dark tomb
  Receives my heart into its quiet keeping,
And some sweet flower begins to bloom
  Above the grassy mound where I am sleeping;
    Ah then, my face thou nevermore shalt see,
    But still my soul will linger close to thee,
      And in the holy place of night,
      The litany of love recite,—
        Remember!

Freely rendered from the French of Alfred de Musset.

"RAPPELLE–TOI"

Remember, when the timid light
  Through the enchanted hall of dawn is gleaming;
Remember, when the pensive night
  Beneath her silver-sprinkled veil walks dreaming;
    When pleasure calls thee and thy heart beats high,
    When tender joys through evening shades draw nigh,
      Hark, from the woodland deeps
      A gentle whisper creeps,
        Remember!

Remember, when the hand of fate
  My life from thine forevermore has parted;
When sorrow, exile, and the weight
  Of lonely years have made me heavy-hearted;
    Think of my loyal love, my last adieu;
    Absence and time are naught, if we are true;
      Long as my heart shall beat,
      To thine it will repeat,
        Remember!

AN HOUR

You only promised me a single hour:
  But in that hour I journeyed through a year
  Of life: the joy of finding you,—the fear
Of losing you again,—the sense of power
To make you all my own,—the sudden shower
  Of tears that came because you were more dear
  Than words could ever tell you,—then,—the clear
Soft rapture when I plucked love's crimson flower.

An hour,—a year,—I felt your bosom rise
  And fall with mystic tides, and saw the gleam
Of undiscovered stars within your eyes,—
  A year,—an hour? I knew not, for the stream
Of love had carried me to Paradise,
  Where all the forms of Time are like a dream.

WITHOUT DISGUISE

If I have erred in showing all my heart,
  And lost your favour by a lack of pride;
  If standing like a beggar at your side
With naked feet, I have forgot the art
Of those who bargain well in passion's mart,
  And win the thing they want by what they hide;
  Be mine the fault as mine the hope denied,
Be mine the lover's and the loser's part.

The sin, if sin it was, I do repent,
  And take the penance on myself alone;
Yet after I have borne the punishment,
  I shall not fear to stand before the throne
Of Love with open heart, and make this plea:
"At least I have not lied to her nor Thee!"

THE BLACK BIRDS

Of beauty from my troubled sight,—
And suddenly it was night!

IV

At break of day I crossed the wooded vale;
And while the morning made
A trembling light among the tree-tops pale,
I saw the sable birds on every limb,
Clinging together closely in the shade,
And croaking placidly their surly hymn.
But, oh, the little land of peace and love
That those night-loving wings had poised above,—
Where was it gone?
Lost, lost, forevermore!
Only a cottage, dull and gray,
In the cold light of dawn,
With iron bars across the door:
Only a garden where the drooping head
Of one sad rose, foreboding its decay,
Hung o'er a barren bed:
Only a desolate field that lay
Untilled beneath the desolate day,—
Where Eden seemed to bloom I found but these!
So, wondering, I passed along my way,
With anger in my heart, too deep for words,
Against that grove of evil-sheltering trees,
And the black magic of the croaking birds.

LABOUR AND ROMANCE

But not too soon! oh, let me linger here
And feed my eyes, hungry with sorrow,
On all this loveliness, so near,
And mine to-morrow!

III

Then, from the wood, across the silvery blue,
A dark bird flew,
Silent, with sable wings.
Close in his wake another came,—
Fragments of midnight floating through
The sunset flame,—
Another and another, weaving rings
Of blackness on the primrose sky,—
Another, and another, look, a score,
A hundred, yes, a thousand rising heavily
From that accursed, dumb, and ancient wood,
They boiled into the lucid air
Like smoke from some deep caldron of despair!
And more, and more, and ever more,
The numberless, ill-omened brood
Flapping their ragged plumes,
Possessed the landscape and the evening light
With menaces and glooms.
Oh, dark, dark, dark they hovered o'er the place
Where once I saw the little house so white
Amid the flowers, covering every trace

THE BLACK BIRDS

I

Once, only once, I saw it clear,—
That Eden every human heart has dreamed
A hundred times, but always far away!
Ah, well do I remember how it seemed,
Through the still atmosphere
Of that enchanted day,
To lie wide open to my weary feet:
A little land of love and joy and rest,
With meadows of soft green,
Rosy with cyclamen, and sweet
With delicate breath of violets unseen,—
And, tranquil 'mid the bloom
As if it waited for a coming guest,
A little house of peace and joy and love
Was nested like a snow-white dove.

II

From the rough mountain where I stood,
Homesick for happiness,
Only a narrow valley and a darkling wood
To cross, and then the long distress
Of solitude would be forever past,—
I should be home at last.

DEPARTURE

Oh, why are you shining so bright, big Sun,
   And why is the garden so gay?
Do you know that my days of delight are done,
   Do you know I am going away?
If you covered your face with a cloud, I'd dream
   You were sorry for me in my pain,
And the heavily drooping flowers would seem
   To be weeping with me in the rain.

But why is your head so low, sweet heart,
   And why are your eyes overcast?
Are you crying because you know we must part,
   Do you think this embrace is our last?
Then kiss me again, and again, and again,
   Look up as you bid me good-bye!
For your face is too dear for the stain of a tear,
   And your smile is the sun in my sky.

ARRIVAL

Across a thousand miles of sea, a hundred leagues of
    land,
Along a path I had not traced and could not understand,
I travelled fast and far for this,—to take thee by the
    hand.

A pilgrim knowing not the shrine where he would bend
    his knee,
A mariner without a dream of what his port would be,
So fared I with a seeking heart until I came to thee.

O cooler than a grove of palm in some heat-weary place,
O fairer than an isle of calm after the wild sea race,
The quiet room adorned with flowers where first I saw
    thy face!

Then furl the sail, let fall the oar, forget the paths of
    foam!
The fate that made me wander far at last has brought
    me home
To thee, dear haven of my heart, and I no more will
    roam.

HESPER

Her eyes are like the evening air,
   Her voice is like a rose,
Her lips are like a lovely song,
   That ripples as it flows,
And she herself is sweeter than
   The sweetest thing she knows.

A slender, haunting, twilight form
   Of wonder and surprise,
She seemed a fairy or a child,
   Till, deep within her eyes,
I saw the homeward-leading star
   Of womanhood arise.

DAY AND NIGHT

How long is the night, brother,
  And how long is the day?
Oh, the day's too short for a happy task,
  And the day's too short for play;
And the night's too short for the bliss of love,—
  For look, how the edge of the sky grows gray,
While the stars die out in the blue above,
  And the wan moon fades away.

How short is the day, brother,
  And how short is the night?
Oh, the day's too long for a heavy task,
  And long, long, long is the night,
When the wakeful hours are filled with pain,
  And the sad heart waits for the thing it fears,
And sighs for the dawn to come again,—
  The night is a thousand years!

How long is a life, dear God,
  And how fast does it flow?
The measure of life is a flame in the soul:
  It is neither swift nor slow.
But the vision of time is the shadow cast
  By the fleeting world on the body's wall;
When it fades there is neither future nor past,
  But love is all in all.

LABOUR AND ROMANCE

For there you stood beside the open door,
Glad, gracious, smiling as before,
And with bright eyes and tender hands outspread
Restored me to the Eden I had lost.
Never a word of cold reproof,
No sharp reproach, no glances that accuse
The culprit whom they hold aloof,—
Ah, 'tis not thus that other women use
The empire they have won!
For there is none like you, belovèd,—none
Secure enough to do what you have done.
Where did you learn this heavenly art,—
You sweetest and most wise of all that live,—
With silent welcome to impart
Assurance of the royal heart
That never questions where it would forgive?

None but a queen could pardon me like this!
My sovereign lady, let me lay
Within each rosy palm a loyal kiss
Of penitence, then close the fingers up,
Thus—thus! Now give the cup
Of full nepenthe in your crimson mouth,
And come—the garden blooms with bliss,
The wind is in the south,
The rose of love with dew is wet—
Dear, it was like you to forget!

NEPENTHE

Yes, it was like you to forget,
And cancel in the welcome of your smile
My deep arrears of debt,
And with the putting forth of both your hands
To sweep away the bars my folly set
Between us—bitter thoughts, and harsh demands,
And reckless deeds that seemed untrue
To love, when all the while
My heart was aching through and through
For you, sweet heart, and only you.

Yet, as I turned to come to you again,
I thought there must be many a mile
Of sorrowful reproach to cross,
And many an hour of mutual pain
To bear, until I could make plain
That all my pride was but the fear of loss,
And all my doubt the shadow of despair
To win a heart so innocent and fair;
And even that which looked most ill
Was but the fever-fret and effort vain
To dull the thirst which you alone could still.

But as I turned, the desert miles were crossed,
And when I came, the weary hours were sped!

THE GENTLE TRAVELLER

"Through many a land your journey ran,
   And showed the best the world can boast:
Now tell me, traveller, if you can,
   The place that pleased you most."

She laid her hands upon my breast,
   And murmured gently in my ear,
"The place I loved and liked the best
   Was in your arms, my dear!"

FIRE-FLY CITY

Many to laugh with me, but never one to know me:
  A cityful of stranger-hearts and none to beat with
      mine!

Look how the glittering lines are wavering and lifting,—
  Softly the breeze of night scatters the vision bright:
      and, passing fair,
Over the meadow-grass and through the forest drifting,
  The Fire-Fly City of the Dark is lost in empty air!

FIRE–FLY CITY

Like a long arrow through the dark the train is darting,
    Bearing me far away, after a perfect day of love's delight:
Wakeful with all the sad-sweet memories of parting,
    I lift the narrow window-shade and look out on the night.

Lonely the land unknown, and like a river flowing,
    Forest and field and hill are gliding backward still athwart my dream;
Till in that country strange, and ever stranger growing,
    A magic city full of lights begins to glow and gleam.

Wide through the landscape dim the lamps are lit in millions;
    Long avenues unfold clear-shining lines of gold across the green;
Clusters and rings of light, and luminous pavilions,—
    Oh, who will tell the city's name, and what these wonders mean?

Why do they beckon me, and what have they to show me?
    Crowds in the blazing street, mirth where the feasters meet, kisses and wine:

A LOVER'S ENVY

I ENVY every flower that blows
Along the meadow where she goes,
  And every bird that sings to her,
  And every breeze that brings to her
    The fragrance of the rose.

I envy every poet's rhyme
That moves her heart at eventime,
  And every tree that wears for her
  Its brightest bloom, and bears for her
    The fruitage of its prime.

I envy every Southern night
That paves her path with moonbeams white,
  And silvers all the leaves for her,
  And in their shadow weaves for her
    A dream of dear delight.

I envy none whose love requires
Of her a gift, a task that tires:
  I only long to live to her,
  I only ask to give to her,
    All that her heart desires.

MY APRIL LADY

When down the stair at morning
  The sunbeams round her float,
Sweet rivulets of laughter
  Are rippling in her throat;
The gladness of her greeting
  Is gold without alloy;
And in the morning sunlight
  I think her name is Joy.

When in the evening twilight
  The quiet book-room lies,
We read the sad old ballads,
  While from her hidden eyes
The tears are falling, falling,
  That give her heart relief;
And in the evening twilight,
  I think her name is Grief.

My little April lady,
  Of sunshine and of showers
She weaves the old spring magic,
  And my heart breaks in flowers!
But when her moods are ended,
  She nestles like a dove;
Then, by the pain and rapture,
  I know her name is Love.

LOVE IN A LOOK

Let me but feel thy look's embrace,
   Transparent, pure, and warm,
And I'll not ask to touch thy face,
   Or fold thee in mine arm.
For in thine eyes a girl doth rise,
   Arrayed in candid bliss,
And draws me to her with a charm
   More close than any kiss.

A loving-cup of golden wine,
   Songs of a silver brook,
And fragrant breaths of eglantine,
   Are mingled in thy look.
More fair they are than any star,
   Thy topaz eyes divine—
And deep within their trysting-nook
   Thy spirit blends with mine.

LABOUR AND ROMANCE

The House of Life is yours, my dear, for many and many
    a day,
But I must ride the lonely shore, the Road to Far Away:
So bring the stirrup-cup and pour a brimming draught,
    I pray,
And when you take the road, my dear, I'll meet you on
    the way.

"RENCONTRE"

Oh, was I born too soon, my dear, or were you born too late,
That I am going out the door while you come in the gate?
For you the garden blooms galore, the castle is *en fête*;
You are the coming guest, my dear,—for me the horses wait.

I know the mansion well, my dear, its rooms so rich and wide;
If you had only come before I might have been your guide,
And hand in hand with you explore the treasures that they hide;
But you have come to stay, my dear, and I prepare to ride.

Then walk with me an hour, my dear, and pluck the reddest rose
Amid the white and crimson store with which your garden glows,—
A single rose,—I ask no more of what your love bestows;
It is enough to give, my dear,—a flower to him who goes.

"UNDINE"

'Twas far away and long ago,
   When I was but a dreaming boy,
This fairy tale of love and woe
   Entranced my heart with tearful joy;
And while with white Undine I wept
   Your spirit,—ah, how strange it seems,—
Was cradled in some star, and slept,
   Unconscious of her coming dreams.

THE ECHO IN THE HEART

It's little I can tell
  About the birds in books;
And yet I know them well,
  By their music and their looks:
      When May comes down the lane,
      Her airy lovers throng
      To welcome her with song,
      And follow in her train:
      Each minstrel weaves his part
      In that wild-flowery strain,
      And I know them all again
      By their echo in my heart.

It's little that I care
  About my darling's place
In books of beauty rare,
  Or heraldries of race:
      For when she steps in view,
      It matters not to me
      What her sweet type may be,
      Of woman, old or new.
      I can't explain the art,
      But I know her for my own,
      Because her lightest tone
      Wakes an echo in my heart.

LOVE'S REASON

For that thy face is fair I love thee not;
   Nor yet because thy brown benignant eyes
   Have sudden gleams of gladness and surprise,
Like woodland brooks that cross a sunlit spot:
Nor for thy body, born without a blot,
   And loveliest when it shines with no disguise
   Pure as the star of Eve in Paradise,—
For all these outward things I love thee not:

But for a something in thy form and face,
   Thy looks and ways, of primal harmony;
A certain soothing charm, a vital grace
   That breathes of the eternal womanly,
And makes me feel the warmth of Nature's breast,
When in her arms, and thine, I sink to rest.

THE CHILD IN THE GARDEN

When to the garden ot untroubled thought
   I came of late, and saw the open door,
   And wished again to enter, and explore
The sweet, wild ways with stainless bloom inwrought,
And bowers of innocence with beauty fraught,
   It seemed some purer voice must speak before
   I dared to tread that garden loved of yore,
That Eden lost unknown and found unsought.

Then just within the gate I saw a child,—
   A stranger-child, yet to my heart most dear;
He held his hands to me, and softly smiled
   With eyes that knew no shade of sin or fear:
"Come in," he said, "and play awhile with me;
"I am the little child you used to be."

DOORS OF DARING

The mountains that inclose the vale
   With walls of granite, steep and high,
Invite the fearless foot to scale
   Their stairway toward the sky.

The restless, deep, dividing sea
   That flows and foams from shore to shore,
Calls to its sunburned chivalry,
   "Push out, set sail, explore!"

The bars of life at which we fret,
   That seem to prison and control,
Are but the doors of daring, set
   Ajar before the soul.

Say not, "Too poor," but freely give;
   Sigh not, "Too weak," but boldly try;
You never can begin to live
   Until you dare to die.

RELIANCE

Not to the swift, the race:
   Not to the strong, the fight:
Not to the righteous, perfect grace
   Not to the wise, the light.

But often faltering feet
   Come surest to the goal;
And they who walk in darkness meet
   The sunrise of the soul.

A thousand times by night
   The Syrian hosts have died;
A thousand times the vanquished right
   Hath risen, glorified.

The truth the wise men sought
   Was spoken by a child;
The alabaster box was brought
   In trembling hands defiled.

Not from my torch, the gleam,
   But from the stars above:
Not from my heart, life's crystal stream,
   But from the depths of Love.

LABOUR AND ROMANCE

III

LIFE

Let me but live my life from year to year,
   With forward face and unreluctant soul;
   Not hurrying to, nor turning from, the goal;
Not mourning for the things that disappear
In the dim past, nor holding back in fear
   From what the future veils; but with a whole
   And happy heart, that pays its toll
To Youth and Age, and travels on with cheer.

So let the way wind up the hill or down,
   O'er rough or smooth, the journey will be joy:
   Still seeking what I sought when but a boy,
New friendship, high adventure, and a crown,
My heart will keep the courage of the quest,
And hope the road's last turn will be the best.

THE THREE BEST THINGS

II

LOVE

Let me but love my love without disguise,
  Nor wear a mask of fashion old or new,
  Nor wait to speak till I can hear a clue,
Nor play a part to shine in others' eyes,
Nor bow my knees to what my heart denies;
  But what I am, to that let me be true,
  And let me worship where my love is due,
And so through love and worship let me rise.

For love is but the heart's immortal thirst
  To be completely known and all forgiven,
  Even as sinful souls that enter Heaven:
So take me, dear, and understand my worst,
And freely pardon it, because confessed,
And let me find in loving thee, my best.

THE THREE BEST THINGS

I

WORK

Let me but do my work from day to day,
  In field or forest, at the desk or loom,
  In roaring market-place or tranquil room;
Let me but find it in my heart to say,
When vagrant wishes beckon me astray,
  "This is my work; my blessing, not my doom;
  "Of all who live, I am the one by whom
"This work can best be done in the right way."

Then shall I see it not too great, nor small,
  To suit my spirit and to prove my powers;
  Then shall I cheerful greet the labouring hours,
And cheerful turn, when the long shadows fall
At eventide, to play and love and rest,
Because I know for me my work is best.

A MILE WITH ME

O who will walk a mile with me
   Along life's merry way?
A comrade blithe and full of glee,
Who dares to laugh out loud and free,
And let his frolic fancy play,
Like a happy child, through the flowers gay
That fill the field and fringe the way
   Where he walks a mile with me.

And who will walk a mile with me
   Along life's weary way?
A friend whose heart has eyes to see
The stars shine out o'er the darkening lea,
And the quiet rest at the end o' the day,—
A friend who knows, and dares to say,
The brave, sweet words that cheer the way
   Where he walks a mile with me.

With such a comrade, such a friend,
I fain would walk till journeys end,
Through summer sunshine, winter rain,
And then?—Farewell, we shall meet again!

LYRICS OF
LABOUR AND ROMANCE

NARRATIVE POEMS

The grass-grown streets were all forlorn,
   The town in ruin stood,
The lady's velvet gown was torn,
   Her rings were sold for food.

Her father had perished long ago,
   But the lady held her pride,
She walked with a scornful step and slow,
   Till at last in her rags she died.

Yet still on the crumbling piers of the town,
   When the midnight moon shines free,
A woman walks in a velvet gown
   And scatters corn in the sea.

1917.

THE PROUD LADY

"Go empty all thy sacks of grain
  Into the nearest sea,
And never show thy face again
  To make a mock of me."

Young Jan Borel, he answered naught,
  But in the harbour cast
The sacks of golden corn he brought,
  And groaned when fell the last.

Then Jan Borel, he hoisted sail,
  And out to sea he bore;
He passed the Helder in a gale
  And came again no more.

But the grains of corn went drifting down
  Like devil-scattered seed,
To sow the harbour of the town
  With a wicked growth of weed.

The roots were thick and the silt and sand
  Were gathered day by day,
Till not a furlong out from land
  A shoal had barred the way.

Then Stävoren town saw evil years,
  No ships could out or in,
The boats lay rotting at the piers,
  And the mouldy grain in the bin.

NARRATIVE POEMS

"Go north and south, go east and west,
    And get me gifts," she said.
"And he who bringeth me home the best,
    With that man will I wed."

So they all fared forth, and sought with care
    In many a famous mart,
For satins and silks and jewels rare,
    To win that lady's heart.

She looked at them all with never a thought,
    And careless put them by;
"I am not fain of the things ye brought,
    Enough of these have I."

The last that came was the head of the fleet,
    His name was Jan Borel;
He bent his knee at the lady's feet,—
    In truth he loved her well.

"I've brought thee home the best i' the world,
    A shipful of Danzig corn!"
She stared at him long; her red lips curled,
    Her blue eyes filled with scorn.

"Now out on thee, thou feckless kerl,
    A loon thou art," she said.
"Am I a starving beggar girl?
    Shall I ever lack for bread?"

THE PROUD LADY

When Stävoren town was in its prime
   And queened the Zuyder Zee,
Her ships went out to every clime
   With costly merchantry.

A lady dwelt in that rich town,
   The fairest in all the land;
She walked abroad in a velvet gown,
   With many rings on her hand.

Her hair was bright as the beaten gold,
   Her lips as coral red,
Her roving eyes were blue and bold,
   And her heart with pride was fed.

For she was proud of her father's ships,
   As she watched them gaily pass;
And pride looked out of her eyes and lips
   When she saw herself in the glass.

"Now come," she said to the captains ten,
   Who were ready to put to sea,
"Ye are all my men and my father's men,
   And what will ye do for me?"

THE STANDARD-BEARER

I

"How can I tell," Sir Edmund said,
  "Who has the right or the wrong o' this thing?
  Cromwell stands for the people's cause,
  Charles is crowned by the ancient laws;
English meadows are sopping red,
Englishmen striking each other dead,—
  Times are black as a raven's wing.
Out of the ruck and the murk I see
    Only one thing!
The King has trusted his banner to me,
  And I must fight for the King."

II

Into the thick of the Edgehill fight
  Sir Edmund rode with a shout; and the ring
  Of grim-faced, hard-hitting Parliament men
  Swallowed him up,—it was one against ten!
He fought for the standard with all his might,
Never again did he come to sight—
  Victor, hid by the raven's wing!
After the battle had passed we found
    Only one thing,—
The hand of Sir Edmund gripped around
  The banner-staff of his King.

1914.

HEROES OF THE "TITANIC"

HONOUR the brave who sleep
   Where the lost "Titanic" lies,
The men who knew what a man must do
   When he looks Death in the eyes.

"Women and children first,"—
   Ah, strong and tender cry!
The sons whom women had borne and nursed,
   Remembered,—and dared to die.

The boats crept off in the dark:
   The great ship groaned: and then,—
O stars of the night, who saw that sight,
   Bear witness, *These were men!*

November 9, 1912.

NARRATIVE POEMS

How they suffered, and struggled, and died, will never be told;
We discovered them all at last when we reached *Gran' Boule* with a boat;
The drowned and the frozen were lyin' stiff and cold,
And the poor little girl with the curls was wrapped in the Captain's coat.

Go write your song of the sea as the landsmen do,
And call her your "great sweet mother," your "bride," and all the rest;
She was made to be loved,—but remember, she won't love you,—
The men who trust her the least are the sailors who know her the best.

"GRAN' BOULE"

He couldn't go back, for he didn't dare to turn;
The sea would have thrown the ship like a mustang
    noosed with a rope;
For the monstrous waves were leapin' high astern,
And the shelter of Seven Island Bay was the only hope.

There's a bunch of broken hills half sunk in the mouth
Of the bay, with their jagged peaks afoam; and the Cap-
    tain thought
He could pass to the north; but the sea kept shovin'
    him south,
With her harlot hands, in the snow-blind murk, till she
    had him caught.

She had waited forty years for a night like this,—
Did he think he could leave her now, and live in a cot-
    tage, the fool?
She headed him straight for the island he couldn't miss;
And heaved his boat in the dark,—and smashed it against
    Gran' Boule.

How the Captain and half of the people clambered
    ashore,
Through the surf and the snow in the gloom of that
    horrible night,
There's no one ever will know. For two days more
The death-white shroud of the tempest covered the
    island from sight.

NARRATIVE POEMS

Now the Holloway Brothers are greedy and thin little men,
With their eyes set close together, and money's their only God;
So they told the Cap' he must run the "Bridget" again,
To fetch a cargo from Moisie, two thousand quintals of cod.

He said the season was over. They said: "Not yet.
You finish the whole of your job, old man, or you don't draw a cent!"
(They had the "Bridget" insured for all they could get.)
And the Captain objected, and cursed, and cried. But he *went*.

They took on the cargo at Moisie, and folks beside,—
Three traders, a priest, and a couple of nuns, and a girl
For a school at Quebec,—when the Captain saw her he sighed,
And said: "Ma littl' Fifi got hair lak' dat, all curl!"

The snow had fallen a foot, and the wind was high,
When the "Bridget" butted her way thro' the billows on Moisie bar.
The darkness grew with the gale, not a star in the sky,
And the Captain swore: "We mus' make *Sept Isles* to-night, by gar!"

"GRAN' BOULE"

"Dose engine one leetl' bit cranky,—too ole, you see,—
She roll and peetch in de wave'. But I lak' 'er pretty well;
An' dat sheep she lak' 'er captaine, sure, dat's me!
Wit' forty ton coal in de bunker, I tek' dat sheep t'rou' hell.

"But I don' wan' risk it no more; I had *bonne chance*:
I save already ten t'ousan' dollar', dat's plenty I s'pose!
Nex' winter I buy dat house wid de garden on France
An' I tell *adieu* to de sea, and I leev' on de lan' in ripose."

All summer he talked of his house,—you could see the flowers
Abloom, and the pear-trees trained on the garden-wall so trim,
And the Captain awalkin' and smokin' away the hours,—
He thought he had done with the sea, but the sea hadn't done with him!

It was late in the fall when he made the last regular run,
Clear down to the Esquimault Point and back with his rickety ship;
She hammered and pounded a lot, for the storms had begun;
But he drove her,—and went for his season's pay at the end of the trip.

NARRATIVE POEMS

You may chance it awhile with the girls like that, if you
    please;
But you want a woman to trust when you settle down
    with a wife;
And a seaman's thought of growin' old at his ease
Is a snug little house on the land to shelter the rest of
    his life.

So that was old Poisson's dream,—did you know the
    Cap'?
A brown little Frenchman, clever, and brave, and quick
    as a fish,—
Had a wife and kids on the other side of the map,—
And a rose-covered cottage for them and him was his
    darlin' wish.

"I 'ave sail," says he, in his broken-up Frenchy talk,
"Mos' forty-two year; I 'ave go on all part of de worl'
    dat ees wet.
I'm seeck of de boat and de water. I rader walk
Wid ma Josephine in one garden; an' eef we get tire',
    we set!

"You see dat *bateau, Sainte Brigitte?* I bring 'er dh'are
From de Breton coas', by gar, jus' feefteen year bifore.
She ole w'en she come on Kebec, but *Holloway Frères*
Dey buy 'er, an' hire me run 'er along dat dam' Nort'
    Shore.

"GRAN' BOULE"

A SEAMAN'S TALE OF THE SEA

WE men that go down for a livin' in ships to the sea,—
We love it a different way from you poets that 'bide on
    the land.
We are fond of it, sure! But, you take it as comin'
    from me,
There's a fear and a hate in our love that a landsman
    can't understand.

Oh, who could help likin' the salty smell, and the blue
Of the waves that are lazily breathin' as if they dreamed
    in the sun?
She's a Sleepin' Beauty, the sea,—but you can't tell
    what she'll do;
And the seamen never trust her,—they know too well
    what she's done!

She's a wench like one that I saw in a singin'-play,—
Carmen they called her,—Lord, what a life her lovers
    did lead!
She'd cuddle and kiss you, and sing you and dance you
    away;
And then,—she'd curse you, and break you, and throw
    you down like a weed.

NARRATIVE POEMS

"And I want your leaves for my five-o'clock tea."
So he ate them all without saying grace,
And walked away with a grin on his face;
While the little tree stood in the twilight dim,
With never a leaf on a single limb.

Then he sighed and groaned; but his voice was weak—
He was so ashamed that he could not speak.
He knew at last he had been a fool,
To think of breaking the forest rule,
And choosing a dress himself to please,
Because he envied the other trees.
But it couldn't be helped, it was now too late,
He must make up his mind to a leafless fate!
So he let himself sink in a slumber deep,
But he moaned and he tossed in his troubled sleep,
Till the morning touched him with joyful beam,
And he woke to find it was all a dream.
For there in his evergreen dress he stood,
A pointed fir in the midst of the wood!
His branches were sweet with the balsam smell,
His needles were green when the white snow fell.
And always contented and happy was he,—
The very best kind of a Christmas tree.

THE FOOLISH FIR-TREE

But a rude young wind through the forest dashed,
In a reckless temper, and quickly smashed
The delicate leaves. With a clashing sound
They broke into pieces and fell on the ground,
Like a silvery, shimmering shower of hail,
And the tree stood naked and bare to the gale.

Then his heart was sad; and he cried, "Alas
"For my beautiful leaves of shining glass!
"Perhaps I have made another mistake
"In choosing a dress so easy to break.
"If the fairies only would hear me again
"I'd ask them for something both pretty and plain:
"It wouldn't cost much to grant my request,—
"In leaves of green lettuce I'd like to be dressed!"
By this time the fairies were laughing, I know;
But they gave him his wish in a second; and so
With leaves of green lettuce, all tender and sweet,
The tree was arrayed, from his head to his feet.
"I knew it!" he cried, "I was sure I could find
"The sort of a suit that would be to my mind.
"There's none of the trees has a prettier dress,
"And none as attractive as I am, I guess."
But a goat, who was taking an afternoon walk,
By chance overheard the fir-tree's talk.
So he came up close for a nearer view;—
"My salad!" he bleated, "I think so too!
"You're the most attractive kind of a tree,

NARRATIVE POEMS

When he woke in the morning, his heart was glad;
For every leaf that his boughs could hold
Was made of the brightest beaten gold.
I tell you, children, the tree was proud;
He was something above the common crowd;
And he tinkled his leaves, as if he would say
To a pedlar who happened to pass that way,
"Just look at me! Don't you think I am fine?
"And wouldn't you like such a dress as mine?"
"Oh, yes!" said the man, "and I really guess
"I must fill my pack with your beautiful dress."
So he picked the golden leaves with care,
And left the little tree shivering there.

"Oh, why did I wish for golden leaves?"
The fir-tree said, "I forgot that thieves
"Would be sure to rob me in passing by.
"If the fairies would give me another try,
"I'd wish for something that cost much less,
"And be satisfied with glass for my dress!"
Then he fell asleep; and, just as before,
The fairies granted his wish once more.
When the night was gone, and the sun rose clear,
The tree was a crystal chandelier;
And it seemed, as he stood in the morning light,
That his branches were covered with jewels bright.
"Aha!" said the tree. "This is something great!"
And he held himself up, very proud and straight;

THE FOOLISH FIR-TREE

A tale that the poet Rückert told
To German children, in days of old;
Disguised in a random, rollicking rhyme
Like a merry mummer of ancient time,
And sent, in its English dress, to please
The little folk of the Christmas trees.

A LITTLE fir grew in the midst of the wood
Contented and happy, as young trees should.
His body was straight and his boughs were clean;
And summer and winter the bountiful sheen
Of his needles bedecked him, from top to root,
In a beautiful, all-the-year, evergreen suit.

But a trouble came into his heart one day,
When he saw that the other trees were gay
In the wonderful raiment that summer weaves
Of manifold shapes and kinds of leaves:
He looked at his needles so stiff and small,
And thought that his dress was the poorest of all.
Then jealousy clouded the little tree's mind,
And he said to himself, "It was not very kind
"To give such an ugly old dress to a tree!
"If the fays of the forest would only ask me,
"I'd tell them how I should like to be dressed,—
"In a garment of gold, to bedazzle the rest!"
So he fell asleep, but his dreams were bad.

NARRATIVE POEMS

And at the monarch's feet spread out his catch—
A hundred salmon, greater than before.
"I win!" he cried: "the King must pay the score."
Then Martin, angry, threw his tackle down:
"Rather than lose this game I'd lose my crown!"
"Nay, thou hast lost them both," the angler said;
And as he spoke a wondrous light was shed
Around his form; he dropped his garments mean,
And in his place the River-god was seen.
"Thy vanity has brought thee in my power,
"And thou must pay the forfeit at this hour:
"For thou hast shown thyself a royal fool,
"Too proud to angle, and too vain to rule,
"Eager to win in every trivial strife,—
"Go! Thou shalt fish for minnows all thy life!"
Wrathful, the King the magic sentence heard;
He strove to answer, but he only *chirr-r-ed:*
His royal robe was changed to wings of blue,
His crown a ruby crest,—away he flew!

So every summer day along the stream
The vain King-fisher darts, an azure gleam,
And scolds the angler with a mocking scream.

April, 1904.

THE VAIN KING

"And catch a hundred larger fish a week—
"Wilt thou accept the challenge, fellow? Speak!"
The angler turned, came near, and bent his knee:
"'Tis not for kings to strive with such as me;
"Yet if the King commands it, I obey.
"But one condition of the strife I pray:
"The fisherman who brings the least to land
"Shall do whate'er the other may command."
Loud laughed the King: "A foolish fisher thou!
'For I shall win, and rule thee then as now."

Then to Prince John, a sober soul, sedate
And slow, King Martin left the helm of State,
While to the novel game with eager zest
He all his time and all his powers addressed.
Sure such a sight was never seen before!
In robe and crown the monarch trod the shore;
His golden hooks were decked with feathers fine,
His jewelled reel ran out a silken line.
With kingly strokes he flogged the crystal stream;
Far-off the salmon saw his tackle gleam;
Careless of kings, they eyed with calm disdain
The gaudy lure, and Martin fished in vain.
On Friday, when the week was almost spent,
He scanned his empty creel with discontent,
Called for a net, and cast it far and wide,
And drew—a thousand minnows from the tide!
Then came the angler to conclude the match,

NARRATIVE POEMS

The nation's wealth was spent in vain display,
And weakness wore the nation's heart away.

Yet think not Earth is blind to human woes—
Man has more friends and helpers than he knows;
And when a patient people are oppressed, .
The land that bore them feels it in her breast.
Spirits of field and flood, of heath and hill,
Are grieved and angry at the spreading ill;
The trees complain together in the night,
Voices of wrath are heard along the height,
And secret vows are sworn, by stream and strand,
To bring the tyrant low and free the land.

But little recked the pampered King of these;
He heard no voice but such as praise and please.
Flattered and fooled, victor in every sport,
One day he wandered idly with his court
Beside the river, seeking to devise
New ways to show his skill to wondering eyes.
There in the stream a patient angler stood,
And cast his line across the rippling flood.
His silver spoil lay near him on the green:
"Such fish," the courtiers cried, "were never seen!
"Three salmon longer than a cloth-yard shaft—
"This man must be the master of his craft!"
"An easy art!" the jealous King replied:
"Myself could learn it better, if I tried,

THE VAIN KING

With which he played at glory's idle game,
To please himself and win the wreaths of fame.
The throne his fathers held from age to age,
To his ambition seemed a fitting stage
Built for King Martin to display at will,
His mighty strength and universal skill.
No conscious child, that, spoiled with praising, tries
At every step to win admiring eyes,
No favourite mountebank, whose acting draws
From gaping crowds the thunder of applause,
Was vainer than the King: his only thirst
Was to be hailed, in every race, the first.
When tournament was held, in knightly guise
The King would ride the lists and win the prize;
When music charmed the court, with golden lyre
The King would take the stage and lead the choir;
In hunting, his the lance to slay the boar;
In hawking, see his falcon highest soar;
In painting, he would wield the master's brush;
In high debate,—"the King is speaking! Hush!"
Thus, with a restless heart, in every field
He sought renown, and made his subjects yield.
But while he played the petty games of life
His kingdom fell a prey to inward strife;
Corruption through the court unheeded crept,
And on the seat of honour justice slept.
The strong trod down the weak; the helpless poor
Groaned under burdens grievous to endure;

THE VAIN KING

In robes of Tyrian blue the King was drest,
A jewelled collar shone upon his breast,
A giant ruby glittered in his crown:
Lord of rich lands and many a splendid town,
In him the glories of an ancient line
Of sober kings, who ruled by right divine,
Were centred; and to him with loyal awe
The people looked for leadership and law.
Ten thousand knights, the safeguard of the land,
Were like a single sword within his hand;
A hundred courts, with power of life and death,
Proclaimed decrees of justice by his breath;
And all the sacred growths that men had known
Of order and of rule upheld his throne.

Proud was the King: yet not with such a heart
As fits a man to play a royal part.
Not his the pride that honours as a trust
The right to rule, the duty to be just:
Not his the dignity that bends to bear
The monarch's yoke, the master's load of care,
And labours like the peasant at his gate,
To serve the people and protect the State.
Another pride was his, and other joys:
To him the crown and sceptre were but toys,

NEW YEAR'S EVE

And smiling so, she laid her palm
In mine. Dear God, it was not cold
But warm with vital heat!
"You live!" I cried, "you live, dear Marguerite!"
Then I awoke; but strangely comforted,
Although I knew again that she was dead.

III

Yes, there's the dream! And was it sweet or sad?
Dear mistress of my waking and my sleep,
Present reward of all my heart's desire,
Watching with me beside the winter fire,
Interpret now this vision that I had.
But while you read the meaning, let me keep
The touch of you: for the Old Year with storm
Is passing through the midnight, and doth shake
The corners of the house,—and oh! my heart would
    break
Unless both dreaming and awake
My hand could feel your hand was warm, warm, warm!
1905.

NARRATIVE POEMS

"I give this song to you."
And then she read:
> *Mein Kind, wir waren Kinder,*
> *Zwei Kinder, jung und froh.*

. . . .

But all the while, a silent question stirred
Within me, though I dared not speak the word:
"Is it herself, and is she truly here,
"And was I dreaming when I heard
"That she was dead last year?
"Or was it true, and is she but a shade
"Who brings a fleeting joy to eye and ear,
"Cold though so kind, and will she gently fade
"When her sweet ghostly part is played
"And the light-curtain falls at dawn of day?"

But while my heart was troubled by this fear
So deeply that I could not speak it out,
Lest all my happiness should disappear,
I thought me of a cunning way
To hide the question and dissolve the doubt.
"Will you not give me now your hand,
"Dear Marguerite," I asked, "to touch and hold,
"That by this token I may understand
"You are the same true friend you were of old?"
She answered with a smile so bright and calm
It seemed as if I saw the morn arise
In the deep heaven of her eyes;

NEW YEAR'S EVE

Amazed, incredulous, confused with joy
I hardly dared to show,
And stammering like a boy,
I took the place she showed me at her side;
And then the talk flowed on with brimming tide
Through the still night,
While she with influence light
Controlled it, as the moon the flood.
She knew where I had been, what I had done,
What work was planned, and what begun;
My troubles, failures, fears she understood,
And touched them with a heart so kind,
That every care was melted from my mind,
And every hope grew bright,
And life seemed moving on to happy ends.
(Ah, what self-beggared fool was he
That said a woman cannot be
The very best of friends?)
Then there were memories of old times,
Recalled with many a gentle jest;
And at the last she brought the book of rhymes
We made together, trying to translate
The Songs of Heine (hers were always best).
"Now come," she said,
"To-night we will collaborate
"Again; I'll put you to the test.
"Here's one I never found the way to do,—
"The simplest are the hardest ones, you know,—

NARRATIVE POEMS

I thought the garden wore
White mourning for her blessed innocence,
And the syringa's breath
Came from the corner by the fence
Where she had made her rustic seat,
With fragrance passionate, intense,
As if it breathed a sigh for Marguerite.
My heart was heavy with a sense
Of something good for ever gone. I sought
Vainly for some consoling thought,
Some comfortable word that I could say
To her sad father, whom I visited again
For the first time since she had gone away.
The bell rang shrill and lonely,—then
The door was opened, and I sent my name
To him,—but ah! 'twas Marguerite who came!
There in the dear old dusky room she stood
Beneath the lamp, just as she used to stand,
In tender mocking mood.
"You did not ask for me," she said,
"And so I will not let you take my hand;
"But I must hear what secret talk you planned
"With father. Come, my friend, be good,
"And tell me your affairs of state:
"Why you have stayed away and made me wait
"So long. Sit down beside me here,—
"And, do you know, it seems a year
"Since we have talked together,—why so late?"

NEW YEAR'S EVE

I

THE other night I had a dream, most clear
And comforting, complete
In every line, a crystal sphere,
And full of intimate and secret cheer.
Therefore I will repeat
That vision, dearest heart, to you,
As of a thing not feigned, but very true,
Yes, true as ever in my life befell;
And you, perhaps, can tell
Whether my dream was really sad or sweet.

II

The shadows flecked the elm-embowered street
I knew so well, long, long ago;
And on the pillared porch where Marguerite
Had sat with me, the moonlight lay like snow.
But she, my comrade and my friend of youth,
Most gaily wise,
Most innocently loved,—
She of the blue-gray eyes
That ever smiled and ever spoke the truth,—
From that familiar dwelling, where she moved
Like mirth incarnate in the years before,
Had gone into the hidden house of Death.

NARRATIVE POEMS

So he travelled onward, desolate no longer, patient in
   his seeking,
  Reaping all the wayside comfort of his quest;
Till at last in Thracia, high upon Mount Hæmus, far from
   human dwelling,
  Weary Aristæus laid him down to rest.

Then the honey-makers, clad in downy whiteness, flut-
   tered soft around him,
  Wrapt him in a dreamful slumber pure and deep.
This is life, beloved: first a sheltered garden, then a
   troubled journey,
  Joy and pain of seeking,—and at last we sleep!

1905.

THE WHITE BEES

Many months he wandered far away in sadness, desolately thinking
    Only of the vanished joys he could not find;
Till the great Apollo, pitying his shepherd, loosed him from the burden
    Of a dark, reluctant, backward-looking mind.

Then he saw around him all the changeful beauty of the changing seasons,
    In the world-wide regions where his journey lay;
Birds that sang to cheer him, flowers that bloomed beside him, stars that shone to guide him,—
    Traveller's joy was plenty all along the way!

Everywhere he journeyed strangers made him welcome, listened while he taught them
    Secret lore of field and forest he had learned:
How to train the vines and make the olives fruitful; how to guard the sheepfolds;
    How to stay the fever when the dog-star burned.

Friendliness and blessing followed in his footsteps; richer were the harvests,
    Happier the dwellings, wheresoe'er he came;
Little children loved him, and he left behind him, in the hour of parting,
    Memories of kindness and a god-like name.

NARRATIVE POEMS

Until, at dawn, the wind lies down
    Weary of fight;
The last torn cloud, with trailing gown,
Passes the open gates of light;
And the white bees are lost in flight.

Look how the landscape glitters wide and still,
    Bright with a pure surprise!
The day begins with joy, and all past ill,
    Buried in white oblivion, lies
Beneath the snow-drifts under crystal skies.
New hope, new love, new life, new cheer,
    Flow in the sunrise beam,—
    The gladness of Apollo when he sees,
Upon the bosom of the wintry year,
The honey-harvest of his wild white bees,
    Forgetfulness and a dream!

III

LEGEND

Listen, my beloved, while the silver morning, like a tranquil vision,
Fills the world around us and our hearts with peace;
Quiet is the close of Aristæus' legend, happy is the ending—
Listen while I tell you how he found release.

THE WHITE BEES

In the desolate day, where no blossoms gleam?
Forgetfulness and a dream!

But now the fretful wind awakes;
I hear him girding at the trees;
He strikes the bending boughs, and shakes
The quiet clusters of the bees
    To powdery drift;
  He tosses them away,
  He drives them like spray;
He makes them veer and shift
  Around his blustering path.
  In clouds blindly whirling,
  In rings madly swirling,
  Full of crazy wrath,
So furious and fast they fly
They blur the earth and blot the sky
    In wild, white mirk.
They fill the air with frozen wings
And tiny, angry, icy stings;
They blind the eyes, and choke the breath,
They dance a maddening dance of death
    Around their work,
Sweeping the cover from the hill,
Heaping the hollows deeper still,
Effacing every line and mark,
And swarming, storming in the dark
    Through the long night;

NARRATIVE POEMS

Now a sudden brightness
Dawns within the sombre day,
Over fields of whiteness;
And the sky is swiftly alive
With the flutter and the flight
Of the shimmering bees, that pour
From the hidden door of the hive
Till you can count no more.

Now on the branches of hemlock and pine
Thickly they settle and cluster and swing,
Bending them low; and the trellised vine
And the dark elm-boughs are traced with a line
Of beauty wherever the white bees cling.
Now they are hiding the wrecks of the flowers,
    Softly, softly, covering all,
Over the grave of the summer hours
    Spreading a silver pall.
Now they are building the broad roof ledge,
Into a cornice smooth and fair,
Moulding the terrace, from edge to edge,
Into the sweep of a marble stair.
Wonderful workers, swift and dumb,
Numberless myriads, still they come,
Thronging ever faster, faster, faster!
Where is their queen? Who is their master?
The gardens are faded, the fields are frore,—
What is the honey they toil to store

THE WHITE BEES

May you hear the humming of the white bee's wing
  Murmur o'er the meadow ere the night bells call.

Wait till winter hardens in the cold gray sky,
  Wait till leaves are fallen and the brooks all freeze,
Then above the gardens where the dead flowers lie,
  Swarm the merry millions of the wild white bees.

> Out of the high-built airy hive,
> Deep in the clouds that veil the sun,
> Look how the first of the swarm arrive;
> Timidly venturing, one by one,
> Down through the tranquil air,
> Wavering here and there,
> Large, and lazy in flight,—
> Caught by a lift of the breeze,
> Tangled among the naked trees,—
> Dropping then, without a sound,
> Feather-white, feather-light,
> To their rest on the ground.
>
> Thus the swarming is begun.
> Count the leaders, every one
> Perfect as a perfect star
> Till the slow descent is done.
> Look beyond them, see how far
> Down the vistas dim and gray,
> Multitudes are on the way.

NARRATIVE POEMS

Lonely Aristæus, sadly home returning, found his garden empty,
   All the hives deserted, all the music fled.

Mournfully bewailing,—"Ah, my honey-makers, where have you departed?"
   Far and wide he sought them over sea and shore;
Foolish is the tale that says he ever found them, brought them home in triumph,—
   Joys that once escape us fly for evermore.

Yet I dream that somewhere, clad in downy whiteness, dwell the honey-makers,
   In aërial gardens that no mortal sees:
And at times returning, lo, they flutter round us, gathering mystic harvest,—
   So I weave the legend of the long-lost bees.

II

THE SWARMING OF THE BEES

Who can tell the hiding of the white bees' nest?
   Who can trace the guiding of their swift home flight?
Far would be his riding on a life-long quest:
   Surely ere it ended would his beard grow white.

Never in the coming of the rose-red Spring,
   Never in the passing of the wine-red Fall,

THE WHITE BEES

I

LEGEND

Long ago Apollo called to Aristæus, youngest of the
    shepherds,
  Saying, "I will make you keeper of my bees."
Golden were the hives and golden was the honey; golden,
    too, the music
  Where the honey-makers hummed among the trees.

Happy Aristæus loitered in the garden, wandered in the
    orchard,
  Careless and contented, indolent and free;
Lightly took his labour, lightly took his pleasure, till the
    fated moment
  When across his pathway came Eurydice.

Then her eyes enkindled burning love within him; drove
    him wild with longing
  For the perfect sweetness of her flower-like face;
Eagerly he followed, while she fled before him, over mead
    and mountain,
  On through field and forest, in a breathless race.

But the nymph, in flying, trod upon a serpent; like a
    dream she vanished;
  Pluto's chariot bore her down among the dead!

NARRATIVE POEMS

He scanned the doubtful task, and muttered "*How?*"
But Asmiel answered, as he turned to go,
With cold, disheartened voice, "I do not know."
. . . .
Now as he went, with fading hope, to seek
The third and last to whom God bade him speak,
Scarce twenty steps away whom should he meet
But Fermor, hurrying cheerful down the street,
With ready heart that faced his work like play,
And joyed to find it greater every day!
The angel stopped him with uplifted hand,
And gave without delay his Lord's command:
"He whom thou servest here would have thee go
"Alone to Spiran's huts, across the snow,
"To serve Him there." Ere Asmiel breathed again
The eager answer leaped to meet him, "*When?*"

The angel's face with inward joy grew bright,
And all his figure glowed with heavenly light;
He took the golden circlet from his brow
And gave the crown to Fermor, answering, "Now!
"For thou hast met the Master's hidden test,
"And I have found the man who loves Him best.
"Not thine, nor mine, to question or reply
"When He commands us, asking 'how?' or 'why?'
"He knows the cause; His ways are wise and just;
"Who serves the King must serve with perfect trust."

February, 1902.

A LEGEND OF SERVICE

The angel's hand:—"The Master bids thee go
"Alone to Spiran's huts, across the snow,
"To serve Him there." Then Bernol's hidden face
Went white as death, and for about the space
Of ten slow heart-beats there was no reply;
Till Bernol looked around and whispered, "*Why?*"
But answer to his question came there none;
The angel sighed, and with a sigh was gone.
. . . .
Within the humble house where Malvin spent
His studious years, on holy things intent,
Sweet stillness reigned; and there the angel found
The saintly sage immersed in thought profound,
Weaving with patient toil and willing care
A web of wisdom, wonderful and fair:
A seamless robe for Truth's great bridal meet,
And needing but one thread to be complete.
Then Asmiel touched his hand, and broke the thread
Of fine-spun thought, and very gently said,
"The One of whom thou thinkest bids thee go
"Alone to Spiran's huts, across the snow,
"To serve Him there." With sorrow and surprise
Malvin looked up, reluctance in his eyes.
The broken thought, the strangeness of the call,
The perilous passage of the mountain-wall,
The solitary journey, and the length
Of ways unknown, too great for his frail strength,
Appalled him. With a doubtful brow

NARRATIVE POEMS

"And well I know who loves me best indeed.
"But every life has pages vacant still,
"Whereon a man may write the thing he will;
"Therefore I read the record, day by day,
"And wait for hearts untaught to learn my way.
"But thou shalt go to Lupon, to the three
"Who serve me there, and take this word from me:
"Tell each of them his Master bids him go
"Alone to Spiran's huts, across the snow;
"There he shall find a certain task for me:
"But what, I do not tell to them nor thee.
"Give thou the message, make my word the test,
"And crown for me the one who loves me best."
Silent the angel stood, with folded hands,
To take the imprint of his Lord's commands;
Then drew one breath, obedient and elate,
And passed the self-same hour, through Lupon's gate.

. . . .

First to the Temple door he made his way;
And there, because it was a holy-day,
He saw the folk in thousands thronging, stirred
By ardent thirst to hear the preacher's word.
Then, while the people whispered Bernol's name,
Through aisles that hushed behind him Bernol came;
Strung to the keenest pitch of conscious might,
With lips prepared and firm, and eyes alight.
One moment at the pulpit step he knelt
In silent prayer, and on his shoulder felt

A LEGEND OF SERVICE

It pleased the Lord of Angels (praise His name!)
To hear, one day, report from those who came
With pitying sorrow, or exultant joy,
To tell of earthly tasks in His employ.
For some were grieved because they saw how slow
The stream of heavenly love on earth must flow;
And some were glad because their eyes had seen,
Along its banks, fresh flowers and living green.
At last, before the whiteness of the throne
The youngest angel, Asmiel, stood alone;
Nor glad, nor sad, but full of earnest thought,
And thus his tidings to the Master brought·
"Lord, in the city Lupon I have found
"Three servants of thy holy name, renowned
"Above their fellows. One is very wise,
"With thoughts that ever range beyond the skies;
"And one is gifted with the golden speech
"That makes men gladly hear when he will teach;
"And one, with no rare gift or grace endued,
"Has won the people's love by doing good.
"With three such saints Lupon is trebly blest;
"But, Lord, I fain would know, which loves Thee best?"
Then spake the Lord of Angels, to whose look
The hearts of all are like an open book:
"In every soul the secret thought I read,

NARRATIVE POEMS

For one by one I'll call my friends to stand beside my bed;
I'll speak the true and tender words so often left unsaid;
And every heart shall throb and glow, all coldness melt away
Around my altar-fire of love—ah, give me but one day!
. . . .
What's that? I've had another day, and wasted it again?
A priceless day in empty dreams, another chance in vain?
Thou fool—this night—it's very dark—the last—this choking breath—
One prayer—have mercy on a dreamer's soul—God, this is death!

ANOTHER CHANCE

Oh, think what it will mean to men, amid their foolish strife,
To see the clear, unshadowed light of one true Christian life,
Without a touch of selfishness, without a taint of sin,—
With one short month of such a life a new world would begin!

. . . .

And love!—I often dream of that—the treasure of the earth;
How little they who use the coin have realised its worth!
'Twill pay all debts, enrich all hearts, and make all joys secure.
But love, to do its perfect work, must be sincere and pure.

My heart is full of virgin gold. I'll pour it out and spend
My hidden wealth with open hand on all who call me friend.
Not one shall miss the kindly deed, the largess of relief,
The generous fellowship of joy, the sympathy of grief.

I'll say the loyal, helpful things that make life sweet and fair,
I'll pay the gratitude I owe for human love and care.
Perhaps I've been at fault sometimes—I'll ask to be forgiven,
And make this little room of mine seem like a bit of heaven.

NARRATIVE POEMS

Who never takes one step aside, nor halts, though hope be dim,
But cleaves a pathway thro' the strife, and bids men follow him.

No blot upon his stainless shield, no weakness in his arm;
No sign of trembling in his face to break his valour's charm:
A man like this could stay the flight and lead the wavering line;
Ah, give me but a year of life—I'll make that glory mine!
. . . .
Religion? Yes, I know it well; I've heard its prayers and creeds,
And seen men put them all to shame with poor, half-hearted deeds.
They follow Christ, but far away; they wander and they doubt.
I'll serve him in a better way, and live his precepts out.

You see, I waited just for this; I could not be content
To own a feeble, faltering faith with human weakness blent.
Too many runners in the race move slowly, stumble, fall;
But I will run so straight and swift I shall outstrip them all.

ANOTHER CHANCE

You'll hear me? Yes, I'm sure you will, my hope is not in vain:
I feel the even pulse of peace, the sweet relief from pain;
The black fog rolls away from me; I'm free once more to plan:
Another chance is all I need to prove myself a man!
. . . .
The world is full of warfare 'twixt the evil and the good;
I watched the battle from afar as one who understood
The shouting and confusion, the bloody, blundering fight—
How few there are that see it clear, how few that wage it right!

The captains flushed with foolish pride, the soldiers pale with fear,
The faltering flags, the feeble fire from ranks that swerve and veer,
The wild mistakes, the dismal doubts, the coward hearts that flee—
The good cause needs a nobler knight to win the victory.

A man whose soul is pure and strong, whose sword is bright and keen,
Who knows the splendour of the fight and what its issues mean;

ANOTHER CHANCE

A DRAMATIC LYRIC

Come, give me back my life again, you heavy-handed Death!
Uncrook your fingers from my throat, and let me draw my breath.
You do me wrong to take me now—too soon for me to die—
Ah, loose me from this clutching pain, and hear the reason why.

I know I've had my forty years, and wasted every one;
And yet, I tell you honestly, my life is just begun;
I've walked the world like one asleep, a dreamer in a trance;
But now you've gripped me wide awake—I want another chance.

My dreams were always beautiful, my thoughts were high and fine;
No life was ever lived on earth to match those dreams of mine.
And would you wreck them unfulfilled? What folly, nay, what crime!
You rob the world, you waste a soul; give me a little time.

VERA

The wandering voice of winds, and underneath
The song of birds, and all the varying tones
Of living things that fill the world with sound,
God spoke to her, and what she heard was peace.

So when the Master questioned, "Dost thou hear?"
She answered, "Yea, at last I hear." And then
He asked her once again, "What hearest thou?
What means the voice of Life?" She answered, "Love!
For love is life, and they who do not love
Are not alive. But every soul that loves,
Lives in the heart of God and hears Him speak."
1898.

Henry Van Dyke

Gone From My Sight

I am standing upon the seashore. I stand and watch her until at length she hangs like a speck of white cloud just where the sea and sky come to mingle with each other.

Then someone at my side says: "There, she is gone!"

"Gone where?"

Gone from my sight. She is just as large in mast and hull and spar as she was when she left my side and she is just as able to bear her load of living freight to her destined port.

Her diminished size is in me, not in her. And just at the moment when someone at my side says: "There, she is gone!"

ready to take up the glad shout: "Here she comes!"

And that is dying.

ECHOES FROM AUGUSTE ANGELLIER

Aurora's virgin whiteness dies
In crimson glory of the skies.

The rapid flame will burn its way
Through these white curtains, too, one day;
The ivory cradle will be left
Undone, and broken, and bereft.

LABOUR AND ROMANCE

II

DREAMS

Often I dream your big blue eyes,
  Though loth their meaning to confess,
Regard me with a clear surprise
  Of dawning tenderness.

Often I dream you gladly hear
  The words I hardly dare to breathe,—
The words that falter in their fear
  To tell what throbs beneath.

Often I dream your hand in mine
  Falls like a flower at eventide,
And down the path we leave a line
  Of footsteps side by side.

But ah, in all my dreams of bliss,
  In passion's hunger, fever's drouth,
I never dare to dream of this:
  My lips upon your mouth.

And so I dream your big blue eyes,
  That look on me with tenderness,
Grow wide, and deep, and sad, and wise,
  And dim with dear distress.

ECHOES FROM AUGUSTE ANGELLIER

III

THE GARLAND OF SLEEP

A wreath of poppy flowers,
  With leaves of lotus blended,
Is carved on Life's façade of hours,
  From night to night suspended.

Along the columned wall,
  From birth's low portal starting,
It flows, with even rise and fall,
  To death's dark door of parting.

How short each measured arc,
  How brief the columns' number!
The wreath begins and ends in dark,
  And leads from sleep to slumber.

The marble garland seems,
  With braided leaf and bloom,
To deck the palace of our dreams
  As if it were a tomb.

LABOUR AND ROMANCE

IV

TRANQUIL HABIT

Dear tranquil Habit, with her silent hands,
  Doth heal our deepest wounds from day to day
  With cooling, soothing oil, and firmly lay
Around the broken heart her gentle bands.

Her nursing is as calm as Nature's care;
  She doth not weep with us; yet none the less
  Her quiet fingers weave forgetfulness,—
We fall asleep in peace when she is there.

Upon the mirror of the mind her breath
  Is like a cloud, to hide the fading trace
  Of that dear smile, of that remembered face,
Whose presence were the joy and pang of death.

And he who clings to sorrow overmuch,
  Weeping for withered grief, has cause to bless,
  More than all cries of pity and distress,—
Dear tranquil Habit, thy consoling touch!

ECHOES FROM AUGUSTE ANGELLIER

V

THE OLD BRIDGE

On the old, old bridge, with its crumbling stones
All covered with lichens red and gray,
Two lovers were talking in sweet low tones:
      And we were they!

As he leaned to breathe in her willing ear
The love that he vowed would never die,
He called her his darling, his dove most dear:
      And he was I!

She covered her face from the pale moonlight
With her trembling hands, but her eyes looked through,
And listened and listened with long delight:
      And she was you!

On the old, old bridge, where the lichens rust,
Two lovers are learning the same old lore;
He tells his love, and she looks her trust:
      But we,—no more!

LABOUR AND ROMANCE

VI

EYES AND LIPS

1

Our silent eyes alone interpreted
  The new-born feeling in the heart of each:
  In yours I read your sorrow without speech,
Your lonely struggle in their tears unshed.
Behind their dreamy sweetness, as a veil,
  I saw the moving lights of trouble shine;
  And then my eyes were brightened as with wine,
My spirit reeled to see your face grow pale!

Our deepening love, that is not yet allowed
  Another language than the eyes, doth learn
To speak it perfectly: above the crowd
Our looks exchange avowals and desires,—
  Like wave-divided beacon lights that burn,
And talk to one another by their fires.

2

When I embrace her in a fragrant shrine
  Of climbing roses, my first kiss shall fall
  On you, sweet eyes, that mutely told me all,—
Through you my soul will rise to make her mine.
Upon your drooping lids, blue-veined and fair,
  The touch of tenderness I first will lay,

ECHOES FROM AUGUSTE ANGELLIER

You springs of joy, lights of my gloomy day,
Whose dear discovered secret bade me dare!

And when you open, eyes of my fond dove,
  Your look will shine with new delight, made sure
By this forerunner of a faithful love.
  'Tis just, dear eyes, so pensive and so pure,
That you should bear the sealing kisses true
Of love unhoped that came to me through you.

3

This was my thought; but when beneath the rose
  That hides the lonely bench where lovers rest,
  In friendly dusk I held her on my breast
For one brief moment,—while I saw you close,
Dear, yielding eyes, as if your lids, blue-veined
  And pure, were meekly fain at last to bear
  The proffered homage of my wistful prayer,—
In that high moment, by your grace obtained,

Forgetting your avowals, your alarms,
  Your anguish and your tears, sweet weary eyes,
Forgetting that you gave her to my arms,
I broke my promise; and my first caress,
  Ungrateful, sought her lips in sweet surprise,—
Her lips, which breathed a word of tenderness!

LABOUR AND ROMANCE

VII

AN EVOCATION

When first upon my brow I felt your kiss,
  A sudden splendour filled me, like the ray
That promptly runs to crown the hills with bliss
  Of purple dawn before the golden day,
And ends the gloom it crosses at one leap.
  My brow was not unworthy your caress;
For some foreboding joy had bade me keep
  From all affront the place your lips would bless.

Yet when your mouth upon my mouth did lay
  The royal touch, no rapture made me thrill,
  But I remained confused, ashamed, and still.
  Beneath your kiss, my queen without a stain,
I felt,—like ghosts who rise at Judgment Day,—
  A throng of ancient kisses vile and vain!

ECHOES FROM AUGUSTE ANGELLIER

VIII

RESIGNATION

1

Well, you will triumph, dear and noble friend!
  The holy love that wounded you so deep
  Will bring you balm, and on your heart asleep
The fragrant dew of healing will descend.
  Your children,—ah, how quickly they will grow
  Between us, like a wall that fronts the sun,
  Lifting a screen with rosy buds o'errun,
To hide the shaded path where I must go.

You'll walk in light; and dreaming less and less
  Of him who droops in gloom beyond the wall,
Your mother-soul will fill with happiness
  When first you hear your grandchild's babbling call,
Beneath the braided bloom of flower and leaf
That life has wrought to veil your vanished grief.

2

Then I alone shall suffer! I shall bear
  The double burden of our grief alone,
While I enlarge my soul to take your share
  Of pain and hold it close beside my own.
Our love is torn asunder; but the crown
  Of thorns that love has woven I will make

LABOUR AND ROMANCE

My relic sacrosanct, and press it down
  Upon my bleeding heart that will not break.

Ah, that will be the depth of solitude!
  For my regret, that evermore endures,
  Will know that new-born hope has conquered yours;
And when the evening comes, no gentle brood
Of wondering children, gathered at my side,
Will soothe away the tears I cannot hide.
Freely rendered from the French, 1911.

RAPPEL D'AMOUR

Come home, my love, come home!
  The twilight is falling,
  The whippoorwill calling,
  The night is very near,
  And the darkness full of fear,
Come home to my arms, come home!

Come home, my love, come home!
  In folly we parted,
  And now, lonely hearted,
  I know you look in vain
  For a love like mine again;
Come home to my arms, come home!

Come home, dear love, come home!
  I've much to forgive you,
  And more yet to give you.
  I'll put a little light
  In the window every night,—
Come home to my arms, come home.

THE RIVER OF DREAMS

The river of dreams runs quietly down
    From its hidden home in the forest of sleep,
    With a measureless motion calm and deep;
And my boat slips out on the current brown,
    In a tranquil bay where the trees incline
    Far over the waves, and creepers twine
    Far over the boughs, as if to steep
    Their drowsy bloom in the tide that goes
    By a secret way that no man knows,
Under the branches bending,
Under the shadows blending,
    And the body rests, and the passive soul
    Is drifted along to an unseen goal,
While the river of dreams runs down.

The river of dreams runs gently down,
    With a leisurely flow that bears my bark
    Out of the visionless woods of dark,
Into a glory that seems to crown
    Valley and hill with light from far,
    Clearer than sun or moon or star,
    Luminous, wonderful, weird, oh, mark
    How the radiance pulses everywhere,
    In the shadowless vault of lucid air!
Over the mountains shimmering,
Up from the fountains glimmering,—

THE RIVER OF DREAMS

    'Tis the mystical glow of the inner light,
    That shines in the very noon of night,
While the river of dreams runs down.

The river of dreams runs murmuring down,
    Through the fairest garden that ever grew;
    And now, as my boat goes drifting through,
A hundred voices arise to drown
    The river's whisper, and charm my ear
    With a sound I have often longed to hear,—
    A magical music, strange and new,
    The wild-rose ballad, the lilac-song,
    The virginal chant of the lilies' throng,
Blue-bells silverly ringing,
Pansies merrily singing,—
    For all the flowers have found their voice;
    And I feel no wonder, but only rejoice,
While the river of dreams runs down.

The river of dreams runs broadening down,
    Away from the peaceful garden-shore,
    With a current that deepens more and more,
By the league-long walls of a mighty town;
    And I see the hurrying crowds of men
    Gather like clouds and dissolve again;
    But never a face I have seen before.
    They come and go, they shift and change,
    Their ways and looks are wild and strange,—

LABOUR AND ROMANCE

This is a city haunted,
A multitude enchanted!
    At the sight of the throng I am dumb with fear,
    And never a sound from their lips I hear,
While the river of dreams runs down.

The river of dreams runs darkly down
    Into the heart of a desolate land,
    With ruined temples half-buried in sand,
And riven hills, whose black brows frown
    Over the shuddering, lonely wave.
    The air grows dim with the dust of the grave;
    No sign of life on the dreary strand;
    No ray of light on the mountain's crest;
    And a weary wind that cannot rest
Comes down the valley creeping,
Lamenting, wailing, weeping,—
    I strive to cry out, but my fluttering breath
    Is choked with the clinging fog of death,
While the river of dreams runs down.

The river of dreams runs trembling down,
    Out of the valley of nameless fear,
    Into a country calm and clear,
With a mystical name of high renown,—
    A name that I know, but may not tell,—
    And there the friends that I loved so well,
    Old companions forever dear,

THE RIVER OF DREAMS

    Come beckoning down to the river shore,
    And hail my boat with the voice of yore.
Fair and sweet are the places
Where I see their unchanged faces!
    And I feel in my heart with a secret thrill,
    That the loved and lost are living still,
While the river of dreams runs down.

The river of dreams runs dimly down
    By a secret way that no man knows;
    But the soul lives on while the river flows
Through the gardens bright and the forests brown;
    And I often think that our whole life seems
    To be more than half made up of dreams.
    The changing sights and the passing shows,
    The morning hopes and the midnight fears,
    Are left behind with the vanished years;
Onward, with ceaseless motion,
The life-stream flows to the ocean,
    While we follow the tide, awake or asleep,
    Till we see the dawn on Love's great deep,
    And the shadows melt, and the soul is free,—
    The river of dreams has reached the sea.

1900.

SONGS OF
HEARTH AND ALTAR

A HOME SONG

I READ within a poet's book
  A word that starred the page:
"Stone walls do not a prison make,
  Nor iron bars a cage!"

Yes, that is true, and something more:
  You'll find, where'er you roam,
That marble floors and gilded walls
  Can never make a home.

But every house where Love abides,
  And Friendship is a guest,
Is surely home, and home-sweet-home:
  For there the heart can rest.

"LITTLE BOATIE"

A SLUMBER-SONG FOR THE FISHERMAN'S CHILD

Furl your sail, my little boatie;
    Here's the haven still and deep,
Where the dreaming tides in-streaming
    Up the channel creep.
Now the sunset breeze is dying;
Hear the plover, landward flying,
Softly down the twilight crying;
    Come to anchor, little boatie,
    In the port of Sleep.

Far away, my little boatie,
    Roaring waves are white with foam;
Ships are striving, onward driving,
    Day and night they roam.
Father's at the deep-sea trawling,
In the darkness, rowing, hauling,
While the hungry winds are calling,—
    God protect him, little boatie,
    Bring him safely home!

Not for you, my little boatie,
    Is the wide and weary sea;
You're too slender, and too tender,
    You must bide with me.

"LITTLE BOATIE"

All day long you have been straying
Up and down the shore and playing;
Come to harbour, no delaying!
    Day is over, little boatie,
        Night falls suddenly.

Furl your sail, my little boatie,
    Fold your wings, my weary dove.
Dews are sprinkling, stars are twinkling
    Drowsily above.
Cease from sailing, cease from rowing;
Rock upon the dream-tide, knowing
Safely o'er your rest are glowing,
    All the night, my little boatie,
        Harbour-lights of love.

1897.

A MOTHER'S BIRTHDAY

Lord Jesus, Thou hast known
  A mother's love and tender care:
    And Thou wilt hear,
      While for my own
    Mother most dear
      I make this birthday prayer.

Protect her life, I pray,
  Who gave the gift of life to me;
    And may she know,
      From day to day,
    The deepening glow
      Of joy that comes from Thee.

As once upon her breast
  Fearless and well content I lay,
    So let her heart,
      On Thee at rest,
    Feel fear depart
      And trouble fade away.

Ah, hold her by the hand,
  As once her hand held mine;
    And though she may
      Not understand
    Life's winding way,
      Lead her in peace divine.

A MOTHER'S BIRTHDAY

I cannot pay my debt
  For all the love that she has given;
    But Thou, love's Lord,
      Wilt not forget
    Her due reward,—
      Bless her in earth and heaven.

TRANSFORMATION

Only a little shrivelled seed,
It might be flower, or grass, or weed;
Only a box of earth on the edge
Of a narrow, dusty window-ledge;
Only a few scant summer showers;
Only a few clear shining hours;
That was all. Yet God could make
Out of these, for a sick child's sake,
A blossom-wonder, fair and sweet
As ever broke at an angel's feet.

Only a life of barren pain,
Wet with sorrowful tears for rain,
Warmed sometimes by a wandering gleam
Of joy, that seemed but a happy dream;
A life as common and brown and bare
As the box of earth in the window there;
Yet it bore, at last, the precious bloom
Of a perfect soul in that narrow room;
Pure as the snowy leaves that fold
Over the flower's heart of gold.

RENDEZVOUS

I COUNT that friendship little worth
   Which has not many things untold,
   Great longings that no words can hold,
And passion-secrets waiting birth.

Along the slender wires of speech
   Some message from the heart is sent;
   But who can tell the whole that's meant?
Our dearest thoughts are out of reach.

I have not seen thee, though mine eyes
   Hold now the image of thy face;
   In vain, through form, I strive to trace
The soul I love: that deeper lies.

A thousand accidents control
   Our meeting here. Clasp hand in hand,
   And swear to meet me in that land
Where friends hold converse soul to soul.

GRATITUDE

"Do you give thanks for this?—or that?" No, God be
    thanked
        I am not grateful
In that cold, calculating way, with blessings ranked
    As one, two, three, and four,—that would be hateful.

I only know that every day brings good above
        My poor deserving;
I only feel that in the road of Life true Love
    Is leading me along and never swerving.

Whatever gifts and mercies to my lot may fall,
        I would not measure
As worth a certain price in praise, or great or small;
    But take and use them all with simple pleasure.

For when we gladly eat our daily bread, we bless
        The Hand that feeds us;
And when we tread the road of Life in cheerfulness,
    Our very heart-beats praise the Love that leads us.

PEACE

With eager heart and will on fire,
I strove to win my great desire.
"Peace shall be mine," I said; but life
Grew bitter in the barren strife.

My soul was weary, and my pride
Was wounded deep; to Heaven I cried,
"God grant me peace or I must die;"
The dumb stars glittered no reply.

Broken at last, I bowed my head,
Forgetting all myself, and said,
"Whatever comes, His will be done;"
And in that moment peace was won.

SANTA CHRISTINA

Saints are God's flowers, fragrant souls
  That His own hand hath planted,
Not in some far-off heavenly place,
  Or solitude enchanted,
But here and there and everywhere,—
  In lonely field, or crowded town,
  God sees a flower when He looks down.

Some wear the lily's stainless white,
  And some the rose of passion,
And some the violet's heavenly blue,
  But each in its own fashion,
With silent bloom and soft perfume,
  Is praising Him who from above
  Beholds each lifted face of love.

One such I knew,—and had the grace
  To thank my God for knowing:
The beauty of her quiet life
  Was like a rose in blowing,
So fair and sweet, so all-complete
  And all unconscious, as a flower,
  That light and fragrance were her dower.

SANTA CHRISTINA

No convent-garden held this rose,
   Concealed like secret treasure;
No royal terrace guarded her
   For some sole monarch's pleasure.
She made her shrine, this saint of mine,
   In a bright home where children played;
   And there she wrought and there she prayed.

In sunshine, when the days were glad,
   She had the art of keeping
The clearest rays, to give again
   In days of rain and weeping;
Her blessed heart could still impart
   Some portion of its secret grace,
   And charity shone in her face.

In joy she grew from year to year;
   And sorrow made her sweeter;
And every comfort, still more kind;
   And every loss, completer.
Her children came to love her name,—
   "Christina,"—'twas a lip's caress;
   And when they called, they seemed to bless.

HEARTH AND ALTAR

No more they call, for she is gone
   Too far away to hear them;
And yet they often breathe her name
   As if she lingered near them;
They cannot reach her with love's speech,
   But when they say "Christina" now
   'Tis like a prayer or like a vow:

A vow to keep her life alive
   In deeds of pure affection,
So that her love shall find in them
   A daily resurrection;
A constant prayer that they may wear
   Some touch of that supernal light
   With which she blossoms in God's sight.

THE BARGAIN

What shall I give for thee,
   Thou Pearl of greatest price?
For all the treasures I possess
   Would not suffice.

I give my store of gold;
   It is but earthly dross:
But thou wilt make me rich, beyond
   All fear of loss.

Mine honours I resign;
   They are but small at best:
Thou like a royal star wilt shine
   Upon my breast.

My worldly joys I give,
   The flowers with which I played;
Thy beauty, far more heavenly fair,
   Shall never fade.

Dear Lord, is that enough?
   Nay, not a thousandth part.
Well, then, I have but one thing more:
   Take Thou my heart.

TO THE CHILD JESUS

I

THE NATIVITY

COULD every time-worn heart but see Thee once again,
A happy human child, among the homes of men,
The age of doubt would pass,—the vision of Thy face
Would silently restore the childhood of the race.

II

THE FLIGHT INTO EGYPT

Thou wayfaring Jesus, a pilgrim and stranger,
   Exiled from heaven by love at thy birth,
Exiled again from thy rest in the manger,
   A fugitive child 'mid the perils of earth,—
Cheer with thy fellowship all who are weary,
   Wandering far from the land that they love;
Guide every heart that is homeless and dreary,
   Safe to its home in thy presence above.

BITTER-SWEET

Just to give up, and trust
    All to a Fate unknown,
Plodding along life's road in the dust,
    Bounded by walls of stone;
Never to have a heart at peace;
Never to see when care will cease;
Just to be still when sorrows fall—
This is the bitterest lesson of all.

Just to give up, and rest
    All on a Love secure,
Out of a world that's hard at the best,
    Looking to heaven as sure;
Ever to hope, through cloud and fear,
In darkest night, that the dawn is near;
Just to wait at the Master's feet—
Surely, now, the bitter is sweet.

HYMN OF JOY

TO THE MUSIC OF BEETHOVEN'S NINTH SYMPHONY

JOYFUL, joyful, we adore Thee,
   God of glory, Lord of love;
Hearts unfold like flowers before Thee,
   Praising Thee their sun above.
Melt the clouds of sin and sadness;
   Drive the dark of doubt away;
Giver of immortal gladness,
   Fill us with the light of day!

All Thy works with joy surround Thee,
   Earth and heaven reflect Thy rays,
Stars and angels sing around Thee,
   Centre of unbroken praise:
Field and forest, vale and mountain,
   Blooming meadow, flashing sea,
Chanting bird and flowing fountain,
   Call us to rejoice in Thee.

Thou art giving and forgiving,
   Ever blessing, ever blest,
Well-spring of the joy of living,
   Ocean-depth of happy rest!
Thou our Father, Christ our Brother,—
   All who live in love are Thine:
Teach us how to love each other,
   Lift us to the Joy Divine.

HYMN OF JOY

Mortals join the mighty chorus,
  Which the morning stars began;
Father-love is reigning o'er us,
  Brother-love binds man to man.
Ever singing march we onward,
  Victors in the midst of strife;
Joyful music lifts us sunward
  In the triumph song of life.

1908.

SONG OF A PILGRIM-SOUL

MARCH on, my soul, nor like a laggard stay!
March swiftly on. Yet err not from the way
Where all the nobly wise of old have trod,—
The path of faith, made by the sons of God.

Follow the marks that they have set beside
The narrow, cloud-swept track, to be thy guide:
Follow, and honour what the past has gained,
And forward still, that more may be attained.

Something to learn, and something to forget:
Hold fast the good, and seek the better yet:
Press on, and prove the pilgrim-hope of youth:
The Creeds are milestones on the road to Truth.

ODE TO PEACE

I

IN EXCELSIS

Two dwellings, Peace, are thine.
  One is the mountain-height,
Uplifted in the loneliness of light
  Beyond the realm of shadows,—fine,
And far, and clear,—where advent of the night
Means only glorious nearness of the stars,
And dawn unhindered breaks above the bars
That long the lower world in twilight keep.
Thou sleepest not, and hast no need of sleep,
For all thy cares and fears have dropped away;
The night's fatigue, the fever-fret of day,
Are far below thee; and earth's weary wars,
  In vain expense of passion, pass
Before thy sight like visions in a glass,—
Or like the wrinkles of the storm that creep
  Across the sea and leave no trace
Of trouble on that immemorial face,—
So brief appear the conflicts, and so slight
The wounds men give, the things for which they fight!
Here hangs a fortress on the distant steep,—
  A lichen clinging to the rock.
There sails a fleet upon the deep,—

HEARTH AND ALTAR

A wandering flock
Of snow-winged gulls. And yonder, in the plain,
A marble palace shines,—a grain
Of mica glittering in the rain.
Beneath thy feet the clouds are rolled
By voiceless winds: and far between
The rolling clouds, new shores and peaks are seen,
In shimmering robes of green and gold,
And faint aerial hue
That silent fades into the silent blue.
Thou, from thy mountain-hold,
All day in tranquil wisdom looking down
On distant scenes of human toil and strife,
All night, with eyes aware of loftier life
Uplifted to the sky where stars are sown,
Dost watch the everlasting fields grow white
Unto the harvest of the sons of light,
And welcome to thy dwelling-place sublime
The few strong souls that dare to climb
The slippery crags, and find thee on the height.

II

DE PROFUNDIS

But in the depth thou hast another home,
For hearts less daring, or more frail.
Thou dwellest also in the shadowy vale;
And pilgrim-souls that roam

ODE TO PEACE

    With weary feet o'er hill and dale,
    Bearing the burden and the heat
       Of toilful days,
      Turn from the dusty ways
To find thee in thy green and still retreat.
    Here is no vision wide outspread
Before the lonely and exalted seat
Of all-embracing knowledge. Here, instead,
A little cottage, and a garden-nook,
    With outlooks brief and sweet
Across the meadows, and along the brook,—
    A little stream that nothing knows
Of the great sea to which it gladly flows,—
A little field that bears a little wheat
To make a portion of earth's daily bread.
    The vast cloud-armies overhead
    Are marshalled, and the wild wind blows
    Its trumpet, but thou canst not tell
Whence comes the wind nor where it goes;
Nor dost thou greatly care, since all is well.
      Thy daily task is done,
And now the wages of repose are won.
Here friendship lights the fire, and every heart,
Sure of itself and sure of all the rest,
Dares to be true, and gladly takes its part
In open converse, bringing forth its best:
And here is music, melting every chain
      Of lassitude and pain:

HEARTH AND ALTAR

And here, at last, is sleep with silent gifts,—
    Kind sleep, the tender nurse who lifts
The soul grown weary of the waking world,
    And lays it, with its thoughts all furled,
Its fears forgotten, and its passions still,
On the deep bosom of the Eternal Will.

THREE PRAYERS FOR SLEEP AND WAKING

I

BEDTIME

Ere thou sleepest gently lay
Every troubled thought away:
Put off worry and distress
As thou puttest off thy dress:
Drop thy burden and thy care
In the quiet arms of prayer.

Lord, Thou knowest how I live,
All I've done amiss forgive:
All of good I've tried to do,
Strengthen, bless, and carry through:
All I love in safety keep,
While in Thee I fall asleep.

HEARTH AND ALTAR

II

NIGHT WATCH

If slumber should forsake
  Thy pillow in the dark,
  Fret not thyself to mark
How long thou liest awake.
There is a better way;
  Let go the strife and strain,
  Thine eyes will close again,
If thou wilt only pray.

Lord, Thy peaceful gift restore,
Give my body sleep once more:
While I wait my soul will rest
Like a child upon Thy breast.

THREE PRAYERS

III

NEW DAY

Ere thou risest from thy bed,
Speak to God Whose wings were spread
O'er thee in the helpless night:
Lo, He wakes thee now with light!
Lift thy burden and thy care
In the mighty arms of prayer.

Lord, the newness of this day
Calls me to an untried way:
Let me gladly take the road,
Give me strength to bear my load,
Thou my guide and helper be—
I will travel through with Thee.

The Mission Inn, California, Easter, 1913.

PORTRAIT AND REALITY

If on the closèd curtain of my sight
  My fancy paints thy portrait far away,
  I see thee still the same, by night or day;
Crossing the crowded street, or moving bright
'Mid festal throngs, or reading by the light
  Of shaded lamp some friendly poet's lay,
  Or shepherding the children at their play,—
The same sweet self, and my unchanged delight.

But when I see thee near, I recognize
  In every dear familiar way some strange
Perfection, and behold in April guise
  The magic of thy beauty that doth range
Through many moods with infinite surprise,—
  Never the same, and sweeter with each change.

THE WIND OF SORROW

The fire of love was burning, yet so low
    That in the peaceful dark it made no rays,
    And in the light of perfect-placid days
The ashes hid the smouldering embers' glow.
Vainly, for love's delight, we sought to throw
    New pleasures on the pyre to make it blaze:
    In life's calm air and tranquil-prosperous ways
We missed the radiant heat of long ago.

Then in the night, a night of sad alarms,
    Bitter with pain and black with fog of fears
That drove us trembling to each other's arms,
    Across the gulf of darkness and salt tears
Into life's calm the wind of sorrow came,
And fanned the fire of love to clearest flame.

HIDE AND SEEK

I

ALL the trees are sleeping, all the winds are still,
All the fleecy flocks of cloud, gone beyond the hill;
Through the noon-day silence, down the woods of June,
Hark, a little hunter's voice, running with a tune.
        "Hide and seek!
        "When I speak,
        "You must answer me:
        "Call again,
        "Merry men,
    "Coo-ee, coo-ee, coo-ee!"

Now I hear his footsteps rustling in the grass:
Hidden in my leafy nook, shall I let him pass?
Just a low, soft whistle,—quick the hunter turns,
Leaps upon me laughing loud, rolls me in the ferns.
        "Hold him fast,
        "Caught at last!
        "Now you're it, you see.
        "Hide your eye,
        "Till I cry,
    Coo-ee, coo-ee, coo-ee!"

HIDE AND SEEK

II

Long ago he left me, long and long ago;
Now I wander thro' the world, seeking high and low.
Hidden safe and happy, in some pleasant place,—
If I could but hear his voice, soon I'd see his face!
    Far away,
    Many a day,
    Where can Barney be?
    Answer, dear,
    Don't you hear?
   Coo-ee, coo-ee, coo-ee!

Birds that every spring-time sung him full of joy,
Flowers he loved to pick for me, mind me of my boy.
Somewhere he is waiting till my steps come nigh;
Love may hide itself awhile, but love can never die.
    Heart, be glad,
    The little lad
    Will call again to thee:
    "Father dear,
    "Heaven is here,
   "Coo-ee, coo-ee, coo-ee!"

1898.

AUTUMN IN THE GARDEN

When the frosty kiss of Autumn in the dark
      Makes its mark
On the flowers, and the misty morning grieves
      Over fallen leaves;
Then my olden garden, where the golden soil
      Through the toil
Of a hundred years is mellow, rich, and deep,
      Whispers in its sleep.

'Mid the crumpled beds of marigold and phlox,
      Where the box
Borders with its glossy green the ancient walks,
      There's a voice that talks
Of the human hopes that bloomed and withered here
      Year by year,—
And the dreams that brightened all the labouring hours,
      Fading as the flowers.

Yet the whispered story does not deepen grief;
      But relief
For the loneliness of sorrow seems to flow
      From the Long-Ago,
When I think of other lives that learned, like mine,
      To resign,
And remember that the sadness of the fall
      Comes alike to all.

AUTUMN IN THE GARDEN

What regrets, what longings for the lost were theirs!
      And what prayers
For the silent strength that nerves us to endure
      Things we cannot cure!
Pacing up and down the garden where they paced,
      I have traced
All their well-worn paths of patience, till I find
      Comfort in my mind.

Faint and far away their ancient griefs appear:
      Yet how near
Is the tender voice, the careworn, kindly face,
      Of the human race!
Let us walk together in the garden, dearest heart,—
      Not apart!
They who know the sorrows other lives have known
      Never walk alone.

October, 1903.

THE MESSAGE

Waking from tender sleep,
  My neighbour's little child
Put out his baby hand to me,
  Looked in my face, and smiled.

It seems as if he came
  Home from a happy land,
To bring a message to my heart
  And make me understand.

Somewhere, among bright dreams,
  A child that once was mine
Has whispered wordless love to him,
  And given him a sign.

Comfort of kindly speech,
  And counsel of the wise,
Have helped me less than what I read
  In those deep-smiling eyes.

Sleep sweetly, little friend,
  And dream again of heaven:
With double love I kiss your hand,—
  Your message has been given.

November, 1903.

DULCIS MEMORIA

Long, long ago I heard a little song,
  (Ah, was it long ago, or yesterday?)
So lowly, slowly wound the tune along,
  That far into my heart it found the way:
A melody consoling and endearing;
And now, in silent hours, I'm often hearing
  The small, sweet song that does not die away.

Long, long ago I saw a little flower—
  (Ah, was it long ago, or yesterday?)
So fair of face and fragrant for an hour,
  That something dear to me it seemed to say,—
A wordless joy that blossomed into being;
And now, in winter days, I'm often seeing
  The friendly flower that does not fade away.

Long, long ago we had a little child,—
  (Ah, was it long ago, or yesterday?)
Into his mother's eyes and mine he smiled
  Unconscious love; warm in our arms he lay.
An angel called! Dear heart, we could not hold him;
Yet secretly your arms and mine infold him—
  Our little child who does not go away.

HEARTH AND ALTAR

Long, long ago? Ah, memory, make it clear—
  (It was not long ago, but yesterday,)
So little and so helpless and so dear—
  Let not the song be lost, the flower decay!
His voice, his waking eyes, his gentle sleeping:
The smallest things are safest in thy keeping,—
  Sweet memory, keep our child with us alway.

November, 1903.

THE WINDOW

All night long, by a distant bell
  The passing hours were notched
On the dark, while her breathing rose and fell;
  And the spark of life I watched
In her face was glowing, or fading,—who could tell?—
  And the open window of the room,
    With a flare of yellow light,
  Was peering out into the gloom,
    Like an eye that searched the night.

*Oh, what do you see in the dark, little window, and why do
  you peer?*
"I see that the garden is crowded with creeping forms of fear:
*Little white ghosts in the locust-tree, wave in the night-wind's
  breath,*
And low in the leafy laurels the lurking shadow of death."

  Sweet, clear notes of a waking bird
    Told of the passing away
  Of the dark,—and my darling may have heard;
    For she smiled in her sleep, while the ray
  Of the rising dawn spoke joy without a word,
    Till the splendour born in the east outburned
      The yellow lamplight, pale and thin,
    And the open window slowly turned
      To the eye of the morning, looking in.

HEARTH AND ALTAR

Oh, what do you see in the room, little window, that makes you so bright?
"I see that a child is asleep on her pillow, soft and white:
With the rose of life on her lips, the pulse of life in her breast,
And the arms of God around her, she quietly takes her rest."

Neuilly, June, 1909.

CHRISTMAS TEARS

The day returns by which we date our years:
Day of the joy of giving,—that means love;
Day of the joy of living,—that means hope;
Day of the Royal Child,—and day that brings
To older hearts the gift of Christmas tears!

Look, how the candles twinkle through the tree,
The children shout when baby claps his hands,
The room is full of laughter and of song!
Your lips are smiling, dearest,—tell me why
Your eyes are brimming full of Christmas tears?

Was it a silent voice that joined the song?
A vanished face that glimmered once again
Among the happy circle round the tree?
Was it an unseen hand that touched your cheek
And brought the secret gift of Christmas tears?

Not dark and angry like the winter storm
Of selfish grief,—but full of starry gleams,
And soft and still that others may not weep,—
Dews of remembered happiness descend
To bless us with the gift of Christmas tears.

HEARTH AND ALTAR

Ah, lose them not, dear heart,—life has no pearls
More pure than memories of joy love-shared.
See, while we count them one by one with prayer,
The Heavenly hope that lights the Christmas tree
Has made a rainbow in our Christmas tears!

1912.

DOROTHEA
1888–1912

A DEEPER crimson in the rose,
A deeper blue in sky and sea,
And ever, as the summer goes,
A deeper loss in losing thee!

A deeper music in the strain
Of hermit-thrush from lonely tree;
And deeper grows the sense of gain
My life has found in having thee.

A deeper love, a deeper rest,
A deeper joy in all I see;
And ever deeper in my breast
A silver song that comes from thee!

Seal Harbour, August 1, 1912.

EPIGRAMS, GREETINGS, AND INSCRIPTIONS

FOR KATRINA'S SUN-DIAL

IN HER GARDEN OF YADDO

Hours fly,
Flowers die
New days,
New ways,
Pass by.
Love stays.

Time is
Too Slow for those who Wait,
Too Swift for those who Fear,
Too Long for those who Grieve,
Too Short for those who Rejoice;
But for those who Love,
Time is not.

FOR KATRINA'S WINDOW

IN HER TOWER OF YADDO

This is the window's message,
    In silence, to the Queen:
"Thou hast a double kingdom
    And I am set between:
Look out and see the glory,
    On hill and plain and sky:
Look in and see the light of love
    That nevermore shall die!"

L'ENVOI

Window in the Queen's high tower,
This shall be thy magic power!
Shut the darkness and the doubt,
Shut the storm and conflict, out;
Wind and hail and snow and rain
Dash against thee all in vain.
Let in nothing from the night,—
Let in every ray of light!

FOR THE FRIENDS AT HURSTMONT

THE HOUSE

The cornerstone in Truth is laid,
The guardian walls of Honour made,
The roof of Faith is built above,
The fire upon the hearth is Love:
Though rains descend and loud winds call,
This happy house shall never fall.

THE HEARTH

When the logs are burning free,
Then the fire is full of glee:
When each heart gives out its best,
Then the talk is full of zest:
Light your fire and never fear,
Life was made for love and cheer.

THE DOOR

The lintel low enough to keep out pomp and pride:
The threshold high enough to turn deceit aside:
The fastening strong enough from robbers to defend:
This door will open at a touch to welcome every friend.

EPIGRAMS AND GREETINGS

THE DIAL
Time can never take
  What Time did not give;
When my shadows have all passed,
  You shall live.

THE SUN-DIAL AT MORVEN

FOR BAYARD AND HELEN STOCKTON

Two hundred years of blessing I record
For Morven's house, protected by the Lord:
And still I stand among old-fashioned flowers
To mark for Morven many sunlit hours.

THE SUN-DIAL AT WELLS COLLEGE

FOR THE CLASS OF 1904

THE shadow by my finger cast
Divides the future from the past:
Before it, sleeps the unborn hour,
In darkness, and beyond thy power:
Behind its unreturning line,
The vanished hour, no longer thine:
One hour alone is in thy hands,—
The NOW on which the shadow stands.

March, 1904.

TO MARK TWAIN

I

AT A BIRTHDAY FEAST

With memories old and wishes new
We crown our cups again,
And here's to you, and here's to you
With love that ne'er shall wane!
And may you keep, at sixty-seven,
The joy of earth, the hope of heaven,
And fame well-earned, and friendship true,
And peace that comforts every pain,
And faith that fights the battle through,
And all your heart's unbounded wealth,
And all your wit, and all your health,—
Yes, here's a hearty health to you,
And here's to you, and here's to you,
Long life to you, Mark Twain.

November 30, 1902.

II

AT THE MEMORIAL MEETING

We knew you well, dear Yorick of the West,
The very soul of large and friendly jest!
You loved and mocked the broad grotesque of things
In this new world where all the folk are kings.

TO MARK TWAIN

Your breezy humour cleared the air, with sport
Of shams that haunt the democratic court;
For even where the sovereign people rule,
A human monarch needs a royal fool.

Your native drawl lent flavour to your wit;
Your arrows lingered but they always hit;
Homeric mirth around the circle ran,
But left no wound upon the heart of man.

We knew you kind in trouble, brave in pain;
We saw your honour kept without a stain;
We read this lesson of our Yorick's years,—
True wisdom comes with laughter and with tears.

November 30, 1910.

STARS AND THE SOUL
(TO CHARLES A. YOUNG, ASTRONOMER)

"Two things," the wise man said, "fill me with awe:
The starry heavens and the moral law."
Nay, add another wonder to thy roll,—
The living marvel of the human soul!

Born in the dust and cradled in the dark,
It feels the fire of an immortal spark,
And learns to read, with patient, searching eyes,
The splendid secret of the unconscious skies.

For God thought Light before He spoke the word;
The darkness understood not, though it heard:
But man looks up to where the planets swim,
And thinks God's thoughts of glory after Him.

What knows the star that guides the sailor's way,
Or lights the lover's bower with liquid ray,
Of toil and passion, danger and distress,
Brave hope, true love, and utter faithfulness?

But human hearts that suffer good and ill,
And hold to virtue with a loyal will,
Adorn the law that rules our mortal strife
With star-surpassing victories of life.

STARS AND THE SOUL

So take our thanks, dear reader of the skies,
Devout astronomer, most humbly wise,
For lessons brighter than the stars can give,
And inward light that helps us all to live.

TO JULIA MARLOWE

(READING KEATS' ODE ON A GRECIAN URN)

Long had I loved this "Attic shape," the brede
Of marble maidens round this urn divine:
But when your golden voice began to read,
The empty urn was filled with Chian wine.

TO JOSEPH JEFFERSON

May 4th, 1898.—To-day, fishing down the Swiftwater, I found Joseph Jefferson on a big rock in the middle of the brook, casting the fly for trout. He said he had fished this very stream three-and-forty years ago; and near by, in the Paradise Valley, he wrote his famous play.—Leaf from my Diary.

We met on Nature's stage,
   And May had set the scene,
With bishop-caps standing in delicate ranks,
And violets blossoming over the banks,
   While the brook ran full between.

The waters rang your call,
   With frolicsome waves a-twinkle,—
They knew you as boy, and they knew you as man,
And every wave, as it merrily ran,
   Cried, "Enter Rip van Winkle!"

THE MOCKING-BIRD

In mirth he mocks the other birds at noon,
Catching the lilt of every easy tune;
But when the day departs he sings of love,—
His own wild song beneath the listening moon.

THE EMPTY QUATRAIN

A FLAWLESS cup: how delicate and fine
The flowing curve of every jewelled line!
Look, turn it up or down, 'tis perfect still,—
But holds no drop of life's heart-warming wine.

PAN LEARNS MUSIC

FOR A SCULPTURE BY SARA GREENE

LIMBER-LIMBED, lazy god, stretched on the rock,
Where is sweet Echo, and where is your flock?
What are you making here? "Listen," said Pan,—
"Out of a river-reed music for man!"

THE SHEPHERD OF NYMPHS

THE nymphs a shepherd took
  To guard their snowy sheep;
He led them down along the brook,
And guided them with pipe and crook,
  Until he fell asleep.

But when the piping stayed,
  Across the flowery mead
The milk-white nymphs ran out afraid:
O Thyrsis, wake! Your flock has strayed,—
  The nymphs a shepherd need.

ECHOES FROM THE GREEK ANTHOLOGY

I

STARLIGHT

With two bright eyes, my star, my love,
Thou lookest on the stars above:
Ah, would that I the heaven might be
With a million eyes to look on thee.

Plato.

II

ROSELEAF

A little while the rose,
And after that the thorn;
An hour of dewy morn,
And then the glamour goes.
Ah, love in beauty born,
A little while the rose!

Unknown.

EPIGRAMS AND GREETINGS

III

PHOSPHOR—HESPER

O morning star, farewell!
My love I now must leave;
The hours of day I slowly tell,
And turn to her with the twilight bell,—
O welcome, star of eve!

Meleager.

IV

SEASONS

Sweet in summer, cups of snow,
Cooling thirsty lips aglow;
Sweet to sailors winter-bound,
Spring arrives with garlands crowned;
Sweeter yet the hour that covers
With one cloak a pair of lovers,
Living lost in golden weather,
While they talk of love together.

Asclepiades.

ECHOES FROM GREEK ANTHOLOGY

V

THE VINE AND THE GOAT

Although you eat me to the root,
I yet shall bear enough of fruit
For wine to sprinkle your dim eyes,
When you are made a sacrifice.

Euenus.

VI

THE PROFESSOR

Seven pupils, in the class
Of Professor Callias,
Listen silent while he drawls,—
Three are benches, four are walls.

Unknown.

ONE WORLD

*"The worlds in which we live are two:
The world 'I am' and the world 'I do.'"*

THE worlds in which we live at heart are one,
The world "I am," the fruit of "I have done";
And underneath these worlds of flower and fruit,
The world "I love,"—the only living root.

JOY AND DUTY

"Joy is a Duty,"—so with golden lore
The Hebrew rabbis taught in days of yore,
And happy human hearts heard in their speech
Almost the highest wisdom man can reach.

But one bright peak still rises far above,
And there the Master stands whose name is Love,
Saying to those whom weary tasks employ:
"Life is divine when Duty is a Joy."

THE PRISON AND THE ANGEL

SELF is the only prison that can ever bind the soul;
Love is the only angel who can bid the gates unroll;
And when he comes to call thee, arise and follow fast;
His way may lie through darkness, but it leads to light
    at last.

THE WAY

WHO seeks for heaven alone to save his soul,
May keep the path, but will not reach the goal;
While he who walks in love may wander far,
But God will bring him where the Blessed are.

LOVE AND LIGHT

There are many kinds of love, as many kinds of light,
And every kind of love makes a glory in the night.
There is love that stirs the heart, and love that gives it rest,
But the love that leads life upward is the noblest and the best.

FACTA NON VERBA

Deeds not Words: I say so too!
And yet I find it somehow true,
A word may help a man in need,
To nobler act and braver deed.

FOUR THINGS

Four things a man must learn to do
If he would make his record true:
To think without confusion clearly;
To love his fellow-men sincerely;
To act from honest motives purely;
To trust in God and Heaven securely.

THE GREAT RIVER

"In la sua volontade è nostra pace."

O mighty river! strong, eternal Will,
Wherein the streams of human good and ill
Are onward swept, conflicting, to the sea!
The world is safe because it floats in Thee.

INSCRIPTION FOR A TOMB IN ENGLAND

READ here, O friend unknown,
  Our grief, of her bereft;
Yet think not tears alone
  Within our hearts are left.
The gifts she came to give,
  Her heavenly love and cheer,
Have made us glad to live
  And die without a fear.

1912.

THE TALISMAN

WHAT is Fortune, what is Fame?
Futile gold and phantom name,—
Riches buried in a cave,
Glory written on a grave.

What is Friendship? Something deep
That the heart can spend and keep:
Wealth that greatens while we give,
Praise that heartens us to live.

Come, my friend, and let us prove
Life's true talisman is love!
By this charm we shall elude
Poverty and solitude.

January 21, 1914.

THORN AND ROSE

FAR richer than a thornless rose
Whose branch with beauty never glows,
Is that which every June adorns
With perfect bloom among its thorns.

Merely to live without a pain
Is little gladness, little gain,
Ah, welcome joy tho' mixt with grief,—
The thorn-set flower that crowns the leaf.

June 20, 1914.

"THE SIGNS"

Dedicated to the Zodiac Club

Who knows how many thousand years ago
The twelvefold Zodiac was made to show
The course of stars above and men below?

The great sun plows his furrow by its "lines":
From all its "houses" mystic meaning shines:
Deep lore of life is written in its "signs."

Aries—Sacrifice.
Snow-white and sacred is the sacrifice
That Heaven demands for what our heart doth prize:
The man who fears to suffer, ne'er can rise.

Taurus—Strength.
Rejoice, my friend, if God has made you strong:
Put forth your force to move the world along:
Yet never shame your strength to do a wrong.

Gemini—Brotherhood.
Bitter his life who lives for self alone,
Poor would he be with riches and a throne:
But friendship doubles all we are and own.

EPIGRAMS AND GREETINGS

Cancer—The Wisdom of Retreat.
Learn from the crab, O runner fresh and fleet,
Sideways to move, or backward, when discreet;
Life is not all advance,—sometimes retreat!

Leo—Fire.
The sign of Leo is the sign of fire.
Hatred we hate: but no man should desire
A heart too cold to flame with righteous ire.

Virgo—Love.
Mysterious symbol, words are all in vain
To tell the secret power by which you reign.
The more we love, the less we can explain.

Libra—Justice.
Examine well the scales with which you weigh;
Let justice rule your conduct every day;
For when you face the Judge you'll need fair play.

Scorpio—Self-Defense.
There's not a creature in the realm of night
But has the wish to live, likewise the right:
Don't tread upon the scorpion, or he'll fight.

Sagittarius—The Archer.
Life is an arrow, therefore you must know
What mark to aim at, how to use the bow,—
Then draw it to the head and let it go!

"THE SIGNS"

Capricornus—The Goat.
The goat looks solemn, yet he likes to run,
And leap the rocks, and gambol in the sun:
The truly wise enjoy a little fun.

Aquarius—Water.
"Like water spilt upon the ground,"—alas,
Our little lives flow swiftly on and pass;
Yet may they bring rich harvests and green grass!

Pisces—The Fishes.
Last of the sacred signs, you bring to me
A word of hope, a word of mystery,—
We all are swimmers in God's mighty sea.
February 28, 1918.

Printed in the United Kingdom
by Lightning Source UK Ltd.
129543UK00001BA/16/A